AN ISLAND LOST

HENRY SHANE

An Island Lost

tellwell

Tellwell Talent
www.tellwell.ca

ISBN
978-1-77302-696-1 (Paperback)
978-1-77302-697-8 (eBook)

Unserer lieben Freundin
und soul mate Irene

Helmut (Henry)

AN ISLAND LOST

INTRODUCTION

The events in this story are all happening on just three islands out of the more than one thousand bigger and smaller ones in the South Pacific. Most of them are uninhabited.

First, there is the island I'm on. It's the biggest in the area and the center of several smaller ones. It has the church, a government office and some stores. The people living on one of the smaller islands do their day-to-day shopping here. To buy bigger and more expensive items, they go to Auckland, the biggest city of New Zealand, a few hours south by plane. Adam lived on this island all his life; Henry, only for two short years, and I'm new here.

The second island is even further north. It, too, is the hub of a wide area, has several churches, a government office and some stores, just like the first. From here, a memorable exodus of half the population took place, about seventy years ago. At the beginning of this story, none of the main characters lives there.

The third island is smaller, about one week away from the second one. This time, the distance is measured by paddling a canoe. There is no air service. Henry was born here. All the characters in the story lived there one summer long. Now it's lost.

CHAPTER 1

Henry had been called Horam as long as he lived on the island, but he had not been back there for about two years, ever since he was banned from it. Today, he was cutting the grass on the bishop's lawn in front of the church.

The bishop was somewhere between fifty and fifty-five years old, overweight, bald, and always sweating. The physical work of running that lawn mower would have done him good, but it was Henry's job.

The owner, or rather administrator of the place, wasn't really a bishop, just an ordinary Catholic priest. About two years ago, he came close to being promoted. Nobody seemed to know why it hadn't been made official yet, but, from that time on, his congregation raised his rank. Bishop was an easy word to pronounce. It united all the older folks, who, many years ago as kids, had played with him in the mud and who knew him as Richard or Dick, with the younger crowd calling him Father.

Yet, many people on this island had been a bit uncomfortable with this term Father. Most still had a birth father. Anyway, there was also God as father to consider. Some non-Catholic people in the village called him Bishop, too, particularly when they expected business. To have a bishop somehow elevated the whole island community, made everybody feel more important.

The lawn was half done when Adam came down the path. He was a few years older than Henry and lived in the main house while Henry had a room on top of the old, unused garage. Why that was, Henry often wondered about. The bishop's house was big enough for him to live there, too, but he wasn't. He went there for meals, but that was it. Henry wasn't envious, though. He was made to believe Adam was the bishop's son, and he just a foster child, not even the bishop's but the society's.

In his two years in the bishop's household, Henry had learned enough about Catholicism to know that priests, including bishops, were not supposed to have children. Maybe the bishop had a family before he became a priest. That must be it, Henry figured. A well-meaning, Christian god would not prevent somebody to follow his calling when it came later in life.

On the other hand, divorces were not being looked upon kindly, either, and so, in Henry's opinion, the bishop's earlier wife, Adam's mother, must have died. A touchy subject, better not to be addressed.

Although almost the same age, the two lads were quite different in appearance. Adam had a slight build with dark, straight hair. He moved quickly and gestured quite a bit with his hands.

Henry was pretty much the opposite. He was much taller with wider shoulders and had Polynesian features. His skin was a bit darker than that of other Polynesians, like the Maoris or Tongans.

"It's going to rain pretty soon," said Adam, looking at the dark clouds, which appeared to be even darker in contrast to the white church tower in front of them. Although having lived in the same household for two years now, the two lads had only recently started talking to each other. In the first year, Henry did not know English well enough. Sure, he started school soon after he was put into foster care, but nobody there spoke his original island's language. Neither did Adam or the bishop.

Henry was placed, quite arbitrarily, into grade three. There he was, at fifteen-years-old, together with nine-year-old little kids, who knew English quite well but knew nothing yet about life. Even if they had been able to communicate, they would have had no common interests to talk about.

Now, two years later and attending school at the senior level, talking to Adam was much better, but he still had to get used to it. Their verbal exchange was not yet a give and take. It was mostly Adam asking questions and Henry answering them, as short as he could.

There was no chronological order to the questions, either, just bits and pieces. Pretty much all of them were related to Henry's past. What Adam got as replies were parts of a puzzle and not many clues as to where they would fit into the whole picture.

It started to rain. Thick and heavy drops came down on them. This was the end of lawn mowing. Cutting wet grass results in a lumpy lawn that might not recover all summer long. The boys had to find cover and right away.

The closest building was the church, but Henry felt an empty, cold, old church was somehow scary. After all, God lived there and might pay them a surprise visit at any time. In their case, it was more likely the bishop would show up, and that would be the end of whatever they were doing or talking about.

They made a run for the old, unused garage, Henry pushing the lawn mower in front of him, back to its station. Except for Henry's room upstairs, the whole building was a collection of dust and spider webs. Upstairs they went.

Adam was following Henry but reluctantly. Henry didn't know it, but Adam had lived there before him. Since Henry's arrival on the scene, he had avoided going there again.

Adam was nineteen-years-old, then. He had been fifteen when he first joined the bishop's household as a foster child, about the same age Henry was, when he arrived.

The bishop had introduced Adam to the congregation as his son. He found a few flowering attributes around this relationship like "my spiritual son," or "my son from god," enough to keep the parishioners from asking too many questions. To Social Services, Adam had been a foster child just like Henry was now.

In fact, the government didn't like the idea of giving a child into the care of a single person—to a single woman, maybe, but not to a single man, and that's what the bishop was, after all.

In response, the bishop formed a society. *Society for the Rescue of Lost Lambs,* it was called, with all the women of the Wednesday women hour as registered members. Social Services still didn't like it but just couldn't think of a way to reject the application, given so many respectable women in town were now foster mothers. Somewhat cautioned, this time the bishop refrained from calling Henry his son.

Adam knew that Henry came from an island some place north and that the boy had been banned by his people not to return. He was found drifting helplessly in the ocean. That was it, not more than that. He just wasn't interested in the other lad before. There might have been some subconscious racial prejudice on Adam's part. If it was, he was fighting it.

"What was the name of the ship that picked you up?" Adam asked after they had made themselves comfortable on the bed. If he knew the name of the vessel, Adam would have a good chance to find out where Henry was picked up and, at least roughly, where the island was he had lived before and was now banned from.

Henry shrugged. "I have no idea. Remember, I didn't even know there was written language."

"What did the ship look like? Was it bigger than the coastguard ship that visits our island sometimes?" Adam suspected it was most likely the coastguard that saved Henry.

"The one that brought me to the big city was about the same size, but the death ship that picked me up first was much bigger."

"You never told me two ships were involved. How come?"

"When they saw me in my canoe, the big one stopped, and they let a little boat down from high up onto the water. At that point I was half dead from dehydration and was falling in and out of consciousness. Nevertheless, I tried to paddle away as fast as I could. I knew I would die soon and end up on this death ship, but I didn't want to speed up the process."

Henry's heart still started racing when he thought of the situation so close to death.

"Exhausted as I was, they just grabbed me and hoisted me and my canoe on deck. The captain was pretty upset because of my attempt to escape, instead of being grateful for the rescue. That's just guessing. I didn't understand a word. Now I know, stopping such a big freighter cost a ton of money. Physically, I was in bad shape, too, and they, therefore, put me into the sick bay."

"Why do you call the ship 'death ship'?" Adam asked.

"A ship with colorful boxes stabled high on deck carries the dead into the next world. Does it not? That's at least what we think on our island."

A container ship obviously, but most of the freighters were carrying containers nowadays. While Adam was thinking of what to do with this sparse information, Henry added, "When this first ship was getting closer to their destination of Auckland, something did go wrong with the machinery. Anyway, it looked as if they were stuck in that place for some time. It was then, close to their final destination, that they must have called the smaller vessel, the coastguard or whoever it was, to take me over."

"If the coastguard was involved at all, we are cooking," said Adam, "they have records of everything they do. With these records, we can find out where they picked you up and what freighter you came from. These people certainly have a log, too, and knowing where they took you on, we have a good chance to find your island. I will write to the coastguard in Auckland."

"Don't bother. I cannot show up on my island again," Henry reminded Adam. "They would stone me as soon as I set a foot on land. Mena and my parents would watch me die and it would break their hearts."

"Who is Mena?"

"My wife, my lover. We would be married by now and live happily together, if it wasn't for Pug."

"Who is Pug, for heaven's sake?"

"The chief of our clan in the village."

"You are talking in puzzles." Adam shook his head. Maybe it was still too early to expect Henry having sorted out his past.

There was the issue of Henry's transfer from Auckland to this island, several hours away by plane. That one, Henry could explain. The coastguard, or whoever it was, had taken him straight to the hospital. His physical health had to be checked out but also his mental health. After all, he was resisting rescue, and during his time on board, he was crying unexplainably most of the time.

The results of all the examinations showed no physical deficiency, but mentally, he was a mess. He wanted to be with his parents and even more so with a certain woman, called Mena, the hospital staff found out, and to be on an island named Koruk. There were lots of women in this big city, ready to comfort a good looking, young fellow and lots of islands in the South Pacific. No Mena and no Koruk, though.

Eventually the experts decided any island would be better for him than the big and bustling city of Auckland. One of the doctors knew the bishop on this island and that the bishop's former foster child, Adam, had reached maturity. There was a vacancy. And that's how Henry came to live with the bishop.

There were many more questions not answered at the time. Henry apologized. "I know; it doesn't make sense now. Someday, I will tell you the story of our people and in the right order. Maybe I will even write it down, once my writing has improved, but going back is out of the question. I just can't, as much as I would like to."

The boys' first real conversation was interrupted when they heard heavy steps coming up the stairs. They both knew it was the bishop coming for one of his personal prayer sessions. Adam quickly left and Henry got ready for a lot of praying, hand-holding, and hugging.

These praying sessions had started quite innocently, sneaking up on Henry, so to speak, over several weeks. There were skills, mostly social skills, Henry didn't learn at school. These skills included how to dress for different occasions, how to use knife and fork and even how to sleep in a bed and not on the floor. Handshaking and other physical contact was also new to him. They didn't do that on the island.

Henry always mimicked the bishop as closely as possible, starting with elaborate greetings when guests arrived and again when they left. There was no end, it seemed to him, for the kissing, hugging, shoulder patting. He just copied it but always felt quite uncomfortable.

Henry figured the importance of good behavior increased as the days progressed. In the morning, a friendly hello was okay in most cases. In contrast, there seemed to be no room for error in the evening.

At school, students and teachers were easygoing. If he did something wrong, they just told him. It was no big deal. At home, however, the bishop was quite fussy about these things. Particularly when he had guests, and that was almost every day.

When the bishop came over to the garage for intense prayer sessions with Henry, it always started out with the same hugging as with guests. It was a bit strange, though, that Henry got such a long and close embrace, when they had seen each other just an hour before.

Once, when the bishop got very excited, Henry wiggled himself out of the embrace. The bishop let him free. A few days later, after church, the bishop asked Henry to watch TV with him, something he had recorded. The video showed another church, where quite a few members of the congregation threw up their arms into the air in excitement. Nevertheless, from then on, the bishop reduced all body contact, and concentrated on praying together. Even that slowly petered out. That day, when the bishop saw Adam leaving, he decided to stop these visits to his foster child altogether, and he did.

CHAPTER 2

Nothing more happened for some time. The two young men ignored for now the issue of Henry's ban and whether he would go back or not. Otherwise, however, they became close friends. Adam slowly helped Henry out of his isolation. He took him to his first baseball game, then signed him up to participate in the school's basketball team. Tall as he was, Henry was very good at it.

Based on his stature and weight, he would have been good at football, too, but didn't like it. On the island, he had learned to avoid any fight. Fighting for fun was beyond his understanding.

They also went bowling together and occasionally ate out at the only fast food outlet. Neither of them had money to do that often, but whenever they did, it was a relief, not to dine at home with the bishop and his guests.

The food at the bishop's house was quite uneven. When guests stayed, food was brought in by a caterer and it was good. With no guests, all three of them raided the fridge whenever they were hungry with no regular meal times. Adam and the bishop sometimes cooked something or stuck frozen food into the microwave. Henry didn't. He just couldn't get over the division of work on the island. There, the women cooked and cleaned the living quarters while the men tended to the fields and went out on the ocean to fish. Why did the bishop not have a housekeeper for the big house? Cleaning at the bishop's place was no problem, though. The cleaning company did it, whenever they cleaned the church. Laundry, everybody did for himself.

Adam was busy with his final exams at school. Finishing school was the main reason why he stayed with the bishop; although, he had turned eighteen a while ago and had shaken off the foster child status. He also spent much time with a socialist youth organization. One of the other members was a blonde girl, with whom he spent a lot of time.

A few months went by, and then occurred this huge convention of the socialist party in Auckland. Adam was sent there by the youth group as their delegate. It was a great honor and Adam was very excited. He had never been away from his birth island. He had never been on an airplane, either. Now, this was one of the rare occasions, when Henry had more experience and could tell him all about it. He had come to the island by plane. There was no other way, considering the huge distances in the South Pacific.

The agenda at the convention included some non-socialist activities for the visitors. One of those was a sight-seeing trip by bus. The driver explained, non-stop, everything they drove by, left and right, by loud speaker, another new experience for Adam. Down on Waterfront Drive, next to the container terminal, the guide pointed out the coastguard station. That reminded Adam of the letter he never wrote. He was here now, so close. He didn't have to write. He could go there.

After the tour, it was still early enough to go back to the harbor and pay a visit to the coast-guard station. He took a cab since he wasn't familiar with the public transportation system. From the cab driver, he learned that the small coastguard office does not normally handle major rescue operations. Those are managed by head office in the capitol, but a small one like picking up Henry, they would.

Back home, when he was about to write to them but never did, Adam had checked out the coastguard on the net. It was mostly a volunteer organization which was somehow connected to the Maritime Rescue Centre, which in turn was connected to RCCNZ, the command center for one of the largest Search and Rescue areas in the world. It comprised the Pacific Ocean North-South between the South Pole and the equator and over to Chili in the east. If necessary, RCC got different types of organizations involved in rescues, like the navy or even civil vessels and planes when they knew these were around the trouble spot. Any one of the container ships in port that day could have initially fished out Henry from the boiling sea, about two years ago. The coastguard, most likely Henry's second ship, was, however, the place to start.

Following the direction, the bus driver had pointed to, he got to a round glass building with all kind of offices in it like Harbour Centre and Maritime Police. Only outside did he detect the word "coastguard" It was written on a rather small white and red pontoon boat moored to the pier. Adam went there and told the one person working on deck his predicament. It was a man, the right age to be the captain, looking very authoritative. He listened carefully but replied, "I'm just cleaning here. You must come back tomorrow morning. The boss should be here around ten o'clock."

Adam realized, it's mostly a volunteer organization, alright.

The next morning's agenda, for which Adam had registered at the convention, was a panel titled "Forms of Democracy." Adam knew a multitude of governments existed all over the globe; everyone called itself a democracy. Some were good, like most of those in Western Europe, but there were some bad ones, too, not at all reflecting the will of the people. He knew there would be some USA-bashing for their flawed electoral system, and he was looking forward to it.

However, his friend Henry was more important now. Adam skipped this lecture and went instead back to the coastguard office by taxi, again. He was there at nine-thirty. And yes, several people were working on the same boat, all looking very busy. One of them talked more than the others. Adam figured he had to be the captain and turned to him.

Before he could say much, the engine started, the lines were taken in and the boat slowly left the pier. "Sorry," called the man from the boat as it quickly gained speed. "We've got to go; there is a rescue situation, and every minute counts."

When Adam walked back, his previous cab was still waiting, the driver hoping Adam wanted to go with him to some other place. Business didn't seem to be good, at least not at ten in the morning when most people were where they wanted to be for the day.

"Can I help you?" the cab driver asked. "You seem to be looking for the coastguard with very little success. I was a volunteer once and my brother still is. Is there anything I can do for you?"

Adam told his story, which was actually Henry's story.

"Well," said the driver, "I fished quite a few guys out of the water when I was still working there. Taking over a native guy from a container-ship, no, I don't remember something like that. Even if I did, I would not know the name of the freighter and where they came from. It would be in the log book, though."

A customer phoned and hired the cab. "I'll be back in twenty minutes," the cab driver said in leaving. "I'll take you to my brother Bill. He might remember the incident. Wait here."

When the cabby came back, he introduced himself to Adam as Wayne, and drove him to Bill's house without saying much. His brother was not yet dressed and in his bathing robe when he opened the door. He had been on duty the night before. Adam recognized him as the person cleaning ship the previous day.

"Roughly in what area was this Henry picked up?" Bill asked. Adam paused. "I don't know." He had thought that taking a native boy and a canoe from a freighter and bringing him here would have been extraordinary enough as to be known to everybody who ever worked there. They would still talk about it in their idle hours, and records of the rescue could be easily found. But Bill just shrugged.

The coastguard volunteers did, in fact, talk about previous rescue operations, when they saved countless lives but not when they just transported somebody who had been saved already to the hospital.

If Henry had been there, he certainly could have given Bill a few more pointers, like how often did the freighter stop on the way here, in how many ports? Was there any cargo besides the containers, and how many nights he was aboard? Things like that. But he wasn't.

Bill phoned several colleagues, asking if they knew anything about either a native boy taken over from a container ship or about a canoe they had picked up at the same time.

After quite a few calls, he was finally successful. A native canoe had been donated by the coastguard to the city's Maritime Museum. "We may find a clue there," he said to Adam and Wayne. "Pour yourself a cup of coffee while I get dressed. We'll go to the museum."

Without stopping at any of the many exhibits, they went straight into one of the side halls where native items were displayed. There, as a centerpiece, although it was just a regular dugout, was a small, wooden canoe. Dried out and not immediately usable, but it was just like Henry had described it to Adam.

On a sign, it said, "Traditional dugout canoe," and in smaller print, "donated by the coastguard." All other exhibit labels showed where the items came from. For this canoe, the museum's administrators obviously didn't know from what region it came. At this point, the visitors didn't know for sure if it was Henry's but the chances of this being his were good.

In the museum's office, they found a binder where all donations were registered. This one was recorded as having been received from the coastguard two years and one month before. This timing was perfect. Off they went in Wayne's cab directly to the coastguard office. Twice somebody on the sidewalk tried to flag the cabby down, but the occupants were on a treasure hunt and not to be stopped.

There, they checked the old records and found an entry from about two years and two months before, "Taken over rescued native boy and a canoe," plus where they did. That port was not very far away from Auckland. No indication as to what ship they had taken the boy over from.

That information didn't help at all. Adam had hoped to find out what freighter Henry had been on and where these people had picked him up originally. Once he knew that, Henry's island would not be far away.

Bill spread out a chart on a large table, designed for that purpose. There were countless islands, bigger ones, smaller ones. A very small one might not even be on the chart, only on one with a larger scale. There wasn't much more Bill could do. He gave Adam some duplicates of the charts they had looked at and Wayne took Adam to his hotel. Maybe the charts helped Henry to remember.

Back home, after the convention, Adam showed the charts to Henry. "My ancestors came originally from a bigger island with a church," he said. "Maybe we can find that island. Our small island would then be only a few days' paddle away."

The bishop came over to have a look. He checked for churches that started out as missionaries' stations. He knew a few, but not all. Then he found a very promising one. A church that was formerly a missionary station, located on one of the larger islands way up north. Somehow the name rang a bell with Henry. This might be the island Social Services had found when they tried to return him to his family. They had used slight nuances in language to locate the area Henry came from but gave up when they learned of the ban.

The bishop phoned. Somebody there knew the history of the place. It turned out, it was, in fact, an island from which there was a memorable exodus of almost all inhabitants about seventy years ago. This was most likely the event, the older people on Henry's island, his ancestors, had talked about so often. Where they went, however, nobody at that far away island with the mission knew.

Henry had been rather passive during the search. When Adam put aside the charts and started searching the vicinity of this island on the computer, using Google Earth, he became more interested. After some time looking at the earth on the monitor, he simply said, "Here it is."

"How can you be sure?" Adam asked, but Henry was.

"If the island you found is my ancestors' home, this bigger island here, where the church is, then this is my smaller island, where I was born. It has the only extinct volcano in the whole area and this island here looks just like it."

Adam took out the respective chart again. The island, that Google's satellite image showed, was marked as uninhabited. It also showed "shallow waters all around" as a warning to shippers. Turning to Henry, he said, "That's why you never had visitors. It reminds me of Robinson Crusoe, who was stranded for many years on an island, not too far from there. All the time he was waiting for somebody to come and rescue him, but nobody did. As opposed to your people, he wanted to be found, your people don't." Adam had read the book out of the bishop's extensive library.

The bishop and Adam got as excited as if they had won the lottery. Henry, however, knew it was like winning the big price, but one that is never paid out. Nothing had changed; he couldn't go back. Accepting that, the bishop was finished with the project of Henry's return. He would not have let his charge go on such a dangerous trip anyway. Social Services would not allow it, either.

Day after day Adam worked on Henry to change his mind and to go back together with him. Finally, Adam played his trump card. "What, if we just visit there, pick up Mena, and leave again, respecting the ban. They can't really object against that." Henry had thought about taking Mena with him when he left there. But it was generally believed banned men would all die. How could he take the woman he loved so much to her certain death? Together with a friend like Adam, having a motorboat and, of course, coming as visitors, it would be quite a different situation.

Piece by piece the youngsters told the bishop of their plan, wanting his approval. They hadn't made much progress, when one day the bishop got a letter from his superior, asking him to appear at a hearing to discuss the status of his foster child and to squelch certain rumours once and for all.

This office received the bishop's prompt response the following day, saying that he was on a missionary journey for which it was too late to call off, particularly since there were two assistants involved and they all had made plans. He would contact the office again as soon as he was back. In the meantime, he would be incommunicado.

All three of them, the bishop, Henry, and Adam went on a flight to Auckland, their starting point, where Henry had arrived after his rescue. During the long plane ride, it was Adam's turn now to tell Henry what to expect there and how busy, in a positive way, Auckland was.

Henry had spent more time in this city than Adam but all of it in the hospital. He hadn't seen anything. Among other excitements, Adam mentioned the sky tower and challenged Henry to jump from the top of it or to do the space walk around it, 192 meters up in the air. That didn't scare Henry at all. Having climbed tall coconut trees almost all his life, fear of heights was unknown to him.

When they arrived, the bishop booked all of them into a small motel, a bit outside the inner city. One room for himself and one next door for the boys. He heard them talking and laughing on their side of the thin wall. Oh, would he have loved to be with these young fellows, but he couldn't. He patted himself on the shoulder for not even trying. When they checked out, he paid for everything as he had done for the flights. Somehow, subconsciously, he felt he would pay for former sins, a medieval indulgence of sorts.

They all went to the harbour looking for a suitable passage, if possible, with the shipping line Henry had been on. Their hope was to find a vessel that would get them at least as far as this former missionary station from where the exodus had taken place. The bishop had not announced his exact arrival there, since he was afraid they might cancel his visit.

But that's exactly what happened. He received mail from that church, to come one month later, for whatever reason. That meant they had to go directly to Henry's island or find a passage to the place where Henry was picked up in the middle of nowhere. From there, they would ideally find the small island, and that only if Henry agreed to go there, which he hadn't yet.

When the bishop thought of his two assistants, he figured that the arrangement to go with the two foster children, who would probably be subject of the hearing, would not strengthen his case. It would be helpful if he had some other people in his group, but Henry insisted, nobody else should know of their mission. Other participants might tell the whole world of his secret island. Like all other people there, he had learned, from childhood on, to avoid contact with the outside world, since it would sooner or later result in war.

That made Wayne the prime candidate to come because he knew of the island already, and so did his brother Bill, to whom Wayne had told everything. Both had no family, which was good, but Bill was invited to a training program with RCCNZ as SARO for the next three months and couldn't join them.

Wayne was delighted about the invitation. He was the adventurous type and always had been. After school, he had joined the navy, hoping for a lot of excitement, but soon did not like the drill. Next, he ran the ferry to Devonport for a while. When that became a routine, he drove the hop-on-hop-off sightseeing bus. That got him into contact with people, something he really enjoyed but only for a while. Then he joined Search and Rescue, full time, sponsored by his brother Bill.

Work was interesting enough, but he needed to earn some money. Wayne was quite wealthy but only asset-rich. He alone had inherited his parents' big house. Bill had received their savings instead. What Wayne lacked was cash to, among other things, maintain this big house.

That's how he came to drive a cab. He figured that was close enough to his previous job as a bus driver. And indeed, the job was even better since he could concentrate on just one passenger or one group of passengers. Bubbly as he was, he always invited his passengers into intense conversations. They in turn used the anonymity of the one-time contact to pour out their heart in front of that stranger. This way, Bill learned of more human fate as he ever could have dreamed of experiencing himself. He was, in fact, writing a book about these encounters with the title of "Stories from the Backseat." A trip to an unexplored volcanic island, together with three interesting characters, was just what he needed.

He hired a driver for his cab, packed a few necessities, and joined the other three within hours.

CHAPTER 3

The original plan was to go to the island first where the mission church was, the place of Henry's ancestors. They would have gone there by plane and then continue by boat to Henry's island.

After the postponement of the bishop's visit there, that plan was now out. A plane ride to the big island would have given them a chance to search for Henry's small island from the air.

Henry's grandfather had always talked about one weeks' paddling, when he told the story of their exodus to all the young people, those born on the island. Later, shortly before his death, he changed the distance to a month. Heroic acts tend to grow as people age.

Flying directly to Henry's island as the next best option was out of the question. Henry was dead against scaring his fellow villagers with a low flying and, eventually, landing plane. On his small island, when very rarely a plane crossed the sky and always way up, the general opinion was they were transportation for the gods, just as container ships were carrying the dead. Anything beyond their understanding, any outside disturbance of their simple life, was made part of their mythology and, therefore, had to be accepted without question. Henry knew by then about the container ships and their real function, and he had been on planes twice and was still alive. But the islanders would fight like devils anybody stepping out of a plane. Thus, they had to go just as Henry had come, but in reverse. First by ship, and then by small boat.

Still in Auckland, they eventually found the shipping line and even the vessel Henry had been on. He did remember what the ship looked like after all. When Adam had first asked him, he could not remember the words written on it. Now he saw the shape, the color of the paint, and even recognized the sound of the engines. Yes, he had been on it.

The crew had changed, but, as expected, there was record of Henry's rescue with the exact position. The closest to Henry's island the big ship would go was the open water where they had picked him up. From there, Henry would find his way home. The stretch he had paddled, he still remembered. They would have to rent a motorboat, though.

Under the circumstances, and being so close to his former home, his parents and to Mena, Henry finally agreed to go back to his island, despite the ban. His new friends would protect him, they assured him, although nobody knew how to do that against a whole village and Pug, the nasty village chief.

The shipping line had a fixed route, a circle of sorts, which they routinely followed every so often. That hadn't changed in the last two years. Henry had been on the ship for the second half of their trip; now he saw the first half, unknown to him.

The negotiations with the shipping company for the fare were difficult. The freighter was not equipped for four passengers. The only spare cabin was the sick bay, the one Henry had been in, but that held only two people. The passengers wanted to get out between two stopping points. This additional stop and launch of the motorboat was costly. It was all doable for the containership company but would interfere with the routine trip of the vessel. However, they sorted it all out, mostly because of the bishop's wide-open wallet.

In the end, the ship did not stop on the high sea as negotiated, simply because the high sea was too high at the time. The four passengers could only launch their little rented motorboat at the nearest port, which was the first one Henry remembered having been to, after his rescue.

That resulted in a much longer distance than what Henry had paddled away from, from his island. And it added a stretch of water he didn't know. There was no way back, though. They had come too far already and had spent too much money.

Once the boat was in the water, they had to get into that unstable thing. The bishop almost fell out again. Then they mounted the outboard. That took a few attempts, all the while the freighter's crew watched from above, full of glee.

Next, the four would-be sailors had to decide who would actually steer. Henry was the only one who had ever been in such a small boat, even smaller ones, but after Adam had started the engine, Henry covered his ears and didn't want to have anything to do with the boat anymore. He wanted his canoe back. Adam reminded him of the lawn mower, which Henry ran expertly. It was in principle the same engine and same sound. In the end, Wayne was steering, Adam working with charts and compass, plotting a course, Henry on the lookout for traffic, and the bishop praying for their lives.

"Hard starboard," Adam was shouting to Wayne, whereupon this land rat promptly steered to the left. "Other side," screamed Adam again. There was quite a bit of traffic, as long as they were close to port. "Around that sailboat," Adam continued his commands.

"Why?" answered Wayne without changing his course. "We were here first." As a cab driver, he was probably thinking of 4-way stops in the city.

"Because sailboats have the right-of-way." Adam grabbed the steering handle and turned the boat around at the last moment. That would have been the end of their journey after just five minutes.

"How come you know all this?" the bishop wondered.

"Because I read the books in your library. There is nothing else to do in your house since watching TV is restricted."

"Some shows, no, with all the violence and the naked girls and the sex. You can always watch nature documentaries, the news, and the Bible hour and, as far I know, you do."

"I do, but the Bible hour—only when there are attractive women hosts. Without them, nobody would watch."

"You'd better watch out here now," Wayne interrupted. "There is this big ship; it is, in fact, our ship, now leaving."

"No problem," said Adam. He was in full control now, the captain, so to speak. "It's going very slow, and there shouldn't be any wake."

As soon as he had finished the sentence, the big ship started her engines in earnest. Water was coming into their boat. "Bail, bail!" Adam screamed. None of the others knew what that was nor was there a bucket or something to do it with. In desperation, Adam grabbed the bishop's hat and started shuffling water. They survived.

Henry was torturing his memory to find the spot where he was picked up by the freighter. He had tried to memorize the big ship's course from the last port to the point, from which he would find his way back, but that was from the deck, high up. Now he was at water level. Everything looked different. Once he had found the spot where he had been picked up, he would find his way back, because he had paddled it. There was no land in sight, just like he had not seen any from his canoe and had to rely on the sun, the current, the wind and flying birds overhead to guess his position. Adam did his best to follow their course on the chart.

Henry wished he had his canoe. This motorboat was wider and faster, but he figured his canoe was much more seaworthy.

Slowly but surely, his comrades became more relaxed. The motor was puttering away, the sea was calm, the sun was shining. There were other freight ships coming their way, but Wayne had learned how to cut their wake rather than face them long side. Besides, these ships were certainly following the same shipping channel that their container ship had followed, and that meant they were on the right course to the point, where Henry had been picked up. From there, he would find the island eventually. The bishop was even hoping, not too soon since he enjoyed the ride. Except for the motor, everything was so peaceful.

There were a few ripples in front of them. "Watch out," said the captain to the helmsman. That was easier said than done. Suddenly, the water was boiling all around them.

Then they saw the first tailfin. Then another one. They were in the middle of a pod of hump back whales. None of the men had ever seen a whale before, but Adam had read about them, Wayne had seen them on TV, and the bishop knew the incredible adventure of Jonas from the Bible. Only Henry had no idea what the creatures were. A big fish or what? The shallow waters around the island kept these monsters always far away. He wished he had his fishing rod with him. There would be meat for everybody in the village and for a long time.

Fascinated, they watched those big mounds with tailfins coming up and diving down. Suddenly, their boat was bumped from below. Not completely lifted out of the water, but far enough for the prop to race at highest speed, without the load. Another bump and the motor stopped. Was this the end of their trip? Did they hit a whale, and was he coming up again for revenge? Adam thought of *Moby Dick*, another book in the bishop's library.

After several fruitless attempts, the motor started again and the whales disappeared. That was the end of their relaxation on the blue water on a sunny day. They all realized how vulnerable they were in that nutshell of a boat on the biggest ocean in the world.

Then they saw land. The island! They were glad to have found it so soon, because it was getting dark. While everybody else was happy, Henry was not. They had landed on the wrong island, just a rock, really, with only a few palm trees. This was not where he came from. Still, they had to quit for the day. Luckily, it was a warm night, like most of them in this part of the world.

Once the stars were out, Henry knew exactly where they had landed. He had never been there, but he knew under what stars his island was, and they weren't too far off. The next morning, they started again and soon reached the right island, without any further difficulties.

Henry's eyes anxiously searched the beach for quite some distance with the engine cut. He was ready to start the engine any time and run. What gave him courage was the expectation of seeing Mena again, no matter what else might happen. Nobody and no manmade structure was visible on the beach, as it was the law. Right behind the beach was the familiar forest of palm trees. He was home. But for how long?

CHAPTER 4

During the two years in which Henry was groomed for life in civilization under guidance of the bishop, Mena was raising her baby, Reila. Shunned by most, she was excluded from the daily distribution of food. Distribution, as it was called, surprisingly in English, was like a farmer's market with individual stands. There were some fruits and vegetables, but it truly was more of a fish market, because mostly seafood was on display. The oddest difference to any market in the big cities was the fact, everything was free. All products were given out according to the needs of families and, of course, the quantity available. Mena had gotten nothing there in a long time but survived on donations from well-meaning neighbors and friends.

Henry's parents would have taken care of her, but they had disappeared the same day Henry was banned and pushed out to sea. They had not been there to say goodbye, which was understandable. It was a heartbreaking situation. Everybody assumed they were somewhere in the bush to be alone with their grief.

When after almost a week, they hadn't come back, a search party was sent out. They didn't find the couple and they didn't find their boat. Checking their hut, the search party noticed several containers together with most of the food out of their earthen storage missing.

Immediately, it was quite clear what had happened. Banned people were sent out right after the verdict with just a little water and no food. Nobody was allowed to join them. Chances for survival were, therefore, close to zero. Henry's parents had obviously tried to follow their son in their canoe with food and water. They could only do that unseen by leaving at night and from the uninhabited side of the island. Chances to meet up with Henry were slim, but it was not as impossible as one would think. The parents assumed their son would not paddle much and eventually end up where the wind and water would carry him. They knew this area, just as Henry did. Mena thought she would never know if that plan had worked out, because the whole family would not come back.

Women, even when they were part of a crime, were never banned like the men. Women were not experienced with the heavy dugout canoes. They would drown for sure, and that would not allow the other islanders to think, it was not the judgement of the court, but the gods deciding the fate of criminals. However, the wives of convicts didn't get any organized community support, including the free distribution of food.

Mena started a little house garden with plants like yam, taro, and manioc. As soon as Reila was old enough to be carried along, she took her deep into the forest to search for fruits like papaya, banana, and bread fruits as well as the occasional edible vegetable like pele.

Some of those had been planted by the first settlers many years ago and had spread into the wild. Even with little around the villages, she always came back with something. Coconuts were plentiful, but somebody had to climb the palm tree and throw them down. Normally a man's job, but Mena had learned to do that, too.

Personal freedom was abundant on the island, except when it came to marriages and children. About two generations before, there was a real threat of overpopulation, similar to the crisis in China, as Henry later on learned in school.

With the same challenge facing them, the two governments took the same corrective measures, without knowing of each other. In the case of the island, the master at the time issued a one-child policy. That was only possible since the women had found out how they could avoid pregnancy by drinking a certain mix of tree juice and herbs, boiled for a long time and then concentrated. This anti-baby brew was very reliable.

When the policy was issued, the ratio of baby boys and baby girls had been about fifty/fifty. Now it mysteriously changed to a majority of baby boys. Could the brew have been adjusted to allow only the desired sex?

The thing was, girls were taught to clean the hut, cook the meals, tend to children and gardens, weave mats, and so on. Boys learned to help their fathers with the hard work, like setting up the huts, preparing the fields, building boats, and fighting the rough seas while fishing. It was quite obvious, in a simple lifestyle with lots of physical work, boys were more important than girls. A boy can learn to do a woman's chores but not many women have the strength to do a man's job.

There is just one thing that girls are better at: they can reproduce. So, once this generation of mostly boys had grown up to be men, there weren't enough women to make a family. The one-child rule was, therefore, changed to two children for each couple. With this rule of now two children, the master still tried to cap the population at the present level, each couple, two people, replacing themselves with two children into the future.

Sweet Reila was an accident, but it was true, the island could not carry an unlimited number of people with the limited resources it had. Food, building materials, even soil, was finite. There had to be a maximum. To divide this overall capacity into limits by clan was probably the best way to keep track of that overall total, but was it fair to the individuals?

The way they avoided inbreeding on such a small island was by arranging marriages. The five chiefs of the five villages decided who is going to marry whom and it has to be somebody from another village. That's how she and Henry got trapped. He was from a different clan all right, and she wanted him. But Pug, the clan chief, wanted her to pick his nephew from yet another clan. Mena insisted on Henry and made the conflict public. That was rebellion against the longstanding custom.

As part of their rebellion, Henry and Mena did something foolish, but something the young mother did not regret. For three beautiful days, they hid in the dense forest, close to the peak of the volcano, and created Reila. Nobody could know about the pregnancy when Henry was dragged before the court. Disappearing with Mena was reason enough for his ban. However, adding to the head count with a baby outside marriage and, therefore, unauthorized, made it worse.

Just a few months ago came a major relief for Mena, a turning point. Another man was punished by eviction. His crime also related to marriage but very different from Henry's. In this new case, the perpetrator had poisoned his older wife in order to marry a younger and, admittedly, very attractive widow.

The murder was discovered and in a lengthy court procedure; with all five clan chiefs and the master present, he was found guilty. The master had no choice but to ban him. There was no prison on the island, and the death penalty was not allowed. Whatever the crime, a guilty verdict was always ban for life and to be pushed out in a canoe. That murder was seen by all as a much bigger crime than Henry's, especially by other older women, afraid for their own lives.

Contrary to Henry's departure, that man tried to come back, away from the deadly current. He was, like most others before him, waiting for the master's pardon. When it didn't come, the flying rocks were better aimed, and he was hit a few times. Wounded as he was, his chances of survival were close to zero.

His would-be wife was now the favorite subject of hate and aggression. She was the top witch.

Mena was the poor subject of a wrong conviction and was allowed to participate at the distribution again. She had enough food now to take some at night to the other woman. Whenever Mena thought of Henry, her lover, and that was every day, she tried to think of a better system than the one they fell victim to.

Mena went to the court proceedings whenever there was one. They were public. There was not much else for entertainment. Never would she have thought of sleeping with another man herself. Too strong was her love for Henry, although, at this point, she had to assume he was dead or at least was unable to come back. None of the banned people ever did. But not yet eighteen, she thought of being with Henry almost every night. Maybe that was the reason for her fascination with love and lust. There was no cure against thoughts. She hated herself for it.

The highest authority on the island was the master. He stood over the five chiefs, the heads of the five villages. The master had sent Henry away but otherwise had not much to do with Mena's fate. Pug, the clan chief, was her adversary. If her clan had had a younger chief, it would probably have been easier, but old Pug did not forgive when somebody crossed his plans—ever. Besides, Mena's unauthorized and unplanned baby screwed up his head count and clan limit.

In general, the decisions of the court were quite fair. The elected chiefs of the villages had to stand before a court of their peers once a year and justify all their decisions. When one failed that test, not only did he lose his job, but his canoe was made ready and out he went, never to be seen again. The master didn't have to justify his own decisions, though. He was there for life.

That was Mena's situation on the island, when one day everybody in the neighborhood rushed to the main beach and dock to look at a rather plumb and noisy boat of an unknown design approaching. That had never happened before, and the onlookers were undecided as to whether they should defend themselves or welcome the strangers. But then, the visitors landed. There were four men in the boat. One of them was Henry.

CHAPTER 5

The boat and the visitors were immediately surrounded by a group of fishermen who had been working on their nets. Mena felt like flying down there and throwing herself into Henry's arms. In the few seconds that she could see him through the crowd, she noticed that he had changed. She had learned, in the meantime, that their short but intense relationship was typical puppy love. He was a grown man now, and she, a mother. Had their love survived?

The villagers were just standing there, unsure of what to do. They recognized Henry but never had a banned person come back. Henry had been away for two years, but he had come back after all. Had that changed anything?

The other three were complete strangers. They even looked a little different, with fairer skin and slightly different features. Come to think of it, the master and some members of his family looked a bit like them, or vice versa. One of them, Wayne, had blond hair, something never seen before.

Instinctively, the crowd was unwelcoming to the strangers. The mood was between neutral and almost hostile. They realized that chances of benefiting from this encounter were rather slim. The strangers had the potential of taking something away from them while, on the other hand, they would not have much to give. Except for four small bags, four heavy yellow jackets and a big red metal box, the boat was rather empty.

Killing them, to get rid of the problem altogether, was not an option. In the absence of wars and living on a small island with no place to hide, hardly any human blood was ever spilled other than in accidents, of which there were many. The ban was the only weapon to keep order, and it worked.

A messenger was sent to the master. He reluctantly ended his morning prayers, put his best robe on, grabbed his cane, and slowly made his way down to the beach. He was almost sixty years old and his running days were behind him.

Also, walking slowly gave him time to think about the situation. He remembered Henry, of course, and the verdict. To send Henry away, again, didn't seem to be a good idea. The three other men, probably his friends, would certainly object and bring him back in their big boat. After all, to come here, they had managed the strong current around the island once already. If they were sent away with Henry, either all four came back again, or, even worse, go back to where they came from and tell everybody about the undiscovered island worth exploring.

The master knew there were other parts of the world and other people, although nobody of the original refugees was alive anymore. All the people living there now were born there. But their ancestors had certainly told them what the outside world looked like. Over the years, some fishermen had been way out and, against all odds, had made it back. Some had even seen people on big ships, some fair-haired, like one of those who had arrived.

The fishermen had told the master about their encounter. The master instinctively felt that there was a risk to their civilization from a contact with other people. Therefore, long ago, the master had converted the sighting to be part of their religion. These ships would carry the dead to heaven, he announced. Lately two ships had been container ships and the reports were of colorful boxes on deck. The boxes became part of the myth and the ashes of the dead were now put into painted boxes and stored in the graveyard in preparation for the eventual transfer to those ships.

The same was true for planes overhead. There weren't many, because the island was not in a flight pass. Whenever one flew overhead, maybe visible but mostly only heard, the villagers took cover under trees and bushes. To them, these planes were the equivalent of UFOs. This way, the planes became part of the myth. There was no need anymore to understand it.

Still slowly walking down to the beach, the master ultimately decided to first welcome the boaters and to offer them anything they needed, but, eventually, he would take their boat away and integrate them into the island's population. To freshen up the genepool would be a real benefit to the community. The master already had a few attractive women in mind. Henry was welcomed, too, because he was the only one to communicate with the strangers.

Henry wanted to meet Mena but couldn't. In fact, they had not yet been able to come close enough for a quick greeting. Foremost on Mena's mind was to show him his daughter. He didn't even know yet, he had one.

All four visitors were stationed in the sick area. There were four huts, one for the medicine man and three for patients. One of those was occupied by three men and one by two women. The third was empty and offered enough space for the visitors.

As they were unpacking their meager belongings, basically a change of cloth and a few personal items, the bishop wondered about payment for rent. He had once stayed in a similar hut in an ocean resort during the only holiday he had ever had. It was primitive, without much furniture, similar to this one. Nevertheless, it was still quite expensive. He had been invited and didn't pay, but he knew how much it was regularly.

He turned to Henry. "How much do you think they will charge us?" None of them planned on staying for more than a few days. Henry wanted to reunite with Mena and was hoping to take her back with him. The bishop wanted to see if any souls could be won for the Christian faith. Wayne had just come for the adventure, without any specific goal. Adam wanted to help his new friend Henry but enjoyed the adventure, like Wayne. So far, his life as a foster child, in several foster homes, had been rather boring, and lately even more so, at the bishop's place.

"No charge," Henry answered. "There is no money to pay with."

"That's impossible." The bishop couldn't believe it, neither did the other two. "What if you need something, some very important item? Let's say a cooking pot."

"There are three ways," explained Henry. "Either you make it for yourself or you make something else and trade or it's given to you for free."

This time Wayne was even more surprised. Outside his short stint at the coastguard, to work for somebody without compensation was something he had never done, with one exception. He had once not charged a woman who had given birth in his cab on the way to the hospital. She left a mess. Later, when she went home with him, in his cab again, she thanked him profusely, introduced her hero to the whole neighborhood, but forgot to pay. He didn't have the heart to remind her. Indirectly, he might have been paid for his generosity, after all, by many later customers, when he told the story again and again during the ride and their admiration was expressed in generous tips. To receive something for free, without payment, was still hard to understand, and both Adam and Wayne decided to bring up that issue again later.

A young woman came in and asked whether they had any requests. She was beautiful and moved graciously, like all young and most older women did on the island. Young Adam's eyes almost rolled out of their sockets, and Wayne was also fascinated. Henry was used to these women, although it had been a while. The hostess reminded him of Mena, and that was no accident. She was, in fact, Mena's sister. The bishop seemed to be completely unaffected and didn't even look twice.

The girl's name was Rona. She soon came back to invite the whites, as they were called now, to move to a table outside. About half a dozen people were already gathered, not just patients but older or crippled men. Rona served a soup. It was hot, which indicated the natives knew how to cook. The soup was brought to the table in a big clay pot. The bishop, already missed his catering service.

He was, however, surprised when he tasted it. The soup was good. "Hey," the bishop commented to the others, "this is no stone age civilization." Henry didn't say anything but grinned from ear to ear.

Once everybody had a filled coconut bowl in front of him, the natives all raised their arms and mumbled something. Henry did, too.

"What was that all about?" the bishop asked.

"We were praying," Henry answered.

The bishop almost spilled his soup in excitement. Here he was among savages, but they did pray before dinner. Amazing.

"To what gods did they pray?"

"They pray to just one god." One god was a major advancement in religions. Nobody knew that better than the bishop. Before the rise of Christianity, most civilizations were pantheistic in some fashion. Most believed in families of gods, who had something to do with the creation of the world and whose members were still in charge of some elements. Others were revering ancestors or both. To see these uncivilized people praying to one god was like a wonder. Had they had contact with missionaries before?

The bishop couldn't stop talking about that mystery to Adam and Henry. Wayne's stance on religion was noncommittal and this was not the time to convert him. Maybe later. Then came the huge disappointment.

"They are not praying to the same god," explained Henry. "Everybody has his own. That's the one they pray to."

There was a long pause among the whites. The natives had overcome their initial surprise by the visit of strangers and were talking about something funny the whole time. What a contrast to the bishop's deep thoughts.

Then the bishop broke the silence. "You can't have a service if everybody has a different god."

"No, we don't," Henry elaborated. "We pray before we eat, when we are by ourselves or in a group, either in the hut or in the forest, and we pray at night."

"You never told me that, Henry." The bishop was upset. "Despite all the services you went to while living in my house, you obviously never accepted Christ."

Henry answered, apologizing, "I always prayed to my personal god in your church. How can one god serve all the people when they have so many contrasting wishes? What if you wish for snow at Christmas, and I hope it doesn't snow because I'm not used to it, and I'm cold? What is the one god going to do?"

Henry knew there would be better examples, things more important than the weather, but he couldn't think of one that moment. The bishop was sure one of his intimate prayer sessions with Henry would straighten him out, but this was not the place for it. In general, he wondered, if his foster child would tolerate the treatment again. He had grown a lot in stature here on the island. The bishop could see quite clearly why, even way back at fifteen, Henry always saw himself as a man. The villagers obviously did, too. They wouldn't have banned a child.

Dinner over, Rona cleared the table, and the two women patients sat down, soon joined by a few old and obviously handicapped other women, just like it was with the men. It was quite clear, men came first in this society, women later, and probably only if food was left. This was not as unusual as the personal gods. There were many cultures in the civilized world with the same view of men being superior and women, lower-ranking. Not something Adam's socialist youth group would have tolerated.

At this time, Henry had already asked Rona about Mena, how she was, and where she lived. Everything was so wide open. She could have died, but she didn't. Thank God. She could have been married to somebody else. She would have had to pick another man, though, and that was very unlikely. Or was it? After all, she had no idea he would come back. She must have assumed he had drowned just like everybody else who had been banned.

Mena was alive. If she wasn't, the whole trip would have been for nothing, at least in Henry's eyes. She was not living with somebody else.

Henry was relieved. There were, of course, the parents, he was concerned about. Henry wondered why he had not yet seen them. It was Rona, again, who gave him the news, bad news this time. The parents had tried to find and rescue him. They were in all likelihood now living somewhere else. They couldn't come back because his father would have been immediately banned.

Late that evening, Henry finally went to Mena's house. She lived in one of these small villages, about a twenty-minute walk from the main community. Rona had not told him about the baby, because she didn't know if it was good or bad news. If Henry didn't love Mena anymore, it was bad news. Mena would have to pick somebody she didn't love or stay single. If they still loved each other, what a story that would be.

Mena had waited all afternoon for Henry to come. She knew he would be needed down there to translate, and in general to help the strangers get settled, but she hoped there would be time afterward. Soon, it was getting dark. Nightfall is very quick and complete in the tropics. She put Reila to bed and extinguished the fire. Would the father of her child still find his way in the dark?

She had almost fallen asleep, when from outside the hut a very familiar voice whispered her name. When she answered, a bright light shone from the entry into the hut, bright as the sun at noon. Against that light and half blinded by it, Mena could only make out Henry's dark outlines. The light disappeared just as quickly as it had come and Henry was all over her. No light required.

In between, Mena wanted to tell Henry of Reila, but it took a while before she had a chance. When she did, he got even more excited. The proud mother tried to describe her features: the full, black hair, the soft skin, the cute little feet, and so on. "You will see for yourself tomorrow, in daylight."

Henry just switched on his very strong flash-light again, something Mena had never seen before, and admired his beautiful daughter right then.

He was about to wake her, take her out of her crib, when Mena stopped him. First of all, the baby needed her sleep, but, secondly, and maybe more importantly, with Reila awake and up, Henry would turn all his attention to her. Mena wanted him a little longer, just for herself. Reila could have him all day tomorrow.

The next morning, Henry had to go back to his comrades. Mena joined him with Reila, because she had to get something at the food distribution. The fishermen, although a bit tired from fishing and fighting the current all morning, distributed everything fairly, according to the number of family members. Some days, there wasn't much to share, but today there was. Mena got a nice big snapper and a few crabs.

Most fish handed out at the distribution were small. Only sporadically did the fishermen catch a tuna or a big marlin. The water around the island was too shallow for these big creatures. Several fishers had to work together to land such a formidable fighter.

Mena would prepare the fish in her earth oven. She had become an expert in cooking this way since no man was in the house to do it. The fish would be enough for her and Reila and her neighbor, a widow, who often didn't want to walk all the way to the distribution. Papayas she had picked herself. Mena didn't expect Henry to be able to join her, and he wasn't.

Rona was at the distribution, too, and received enough food for the sick, the old and, of course, for her new charges, the whites. She was all smiles when she saw Henry, Mena, and Reila happily together.

CHAPTER 6

While Mena went home with Reila, carrying the fish in a basket, Henry joined the people at the hospital again, where breakfast was in full swing. The food was basically the same as the evening before. There were only two meals a day everywhere on the island, and the food was always mostly fish with a large variety of fruits. Between meals, a basket with papayas, bananas, and other fruit was always on the table.

Once finished, Henry gathered his crew for a tour of the island. They had already pretty much seen everything that was to be seen in the main village. They had also seen, if only from afar, the master's houses between huge Palm trees up on the hill with the open area for the court next to them. It was not in session. The hill was connected to the first village by an aqueduct as in Roman times, to supply water to the hill across the dip in between.

The other public building was the daycare for babies and little children. Mothers deposited their small children there on days when they were making tapa. There weren't enough mulberry trees on the island and they had to work with other trees, which was hard, but they did it as a group. They also used the daycare when they were doing laundry by the creek for the few textiles they still cherished.

Next, the whites walked up the trail to the five villages. These were much smaller than the main place, with only four or five houses each. To spread out the villages over half a mile or so gave everybody enough space to have a garden.

Some had small, pigeon-like birds running around the hut. Since there were no fences, their wings were clipped. The birds were not as big as grocery store chickens in the city, but that was all there was. Mena didn't have any. Doing all the work by herself, which normally was done by a couple, she just didn't have the time to care for them.

The villages were all situated close to the creek, like pearls on a string. Everybody was very careful with the creek's water, not to spoil it, since they drank it as it was. Since water was so critical for their whole existence, somebody was put in charge of it at all times.

There was a cache, a basin, by which the water flow was controlled. In times of plenty, the basin filled itself to the rim and the surplus ran down. When there was little or no natural flow, the dike was partially or completely opened to allow water to run in the creek. When the basin was completely dry, the water manager had to take water out of a deep well with buckets and either fill the basin or take it directly to the individual houses. That was rare, but it changed an otherwise easy job into real work.

The sightseeing team came also by the graveyard with colorful wooden boxes for the ashes.

Henry pointed at them. Adam nodded. He understood. This here was the origin of the death ship Henry was talking about at home. Henry himself had always wondered how the deceased would make it from there to the ships and eventually to heaven. Having been on such a containership made such a trip even more mysterious.

When the party arrived at the last of the villages, Henry saw Mena and Reila outside their hut and decided to play with his daughter rather than guide his group any further. They had walked as far as the main trail went, there was not much more. The terrain became increasingly steep. Next was the flank of the inactive volcano. This was, where the individual gods lived, and it was strictly off limits to humans. If somebody was seen there, well, we know by now what the punishment would have been.

With Henry away, the three whites pondered what the next steps would be. Wayne and Henry were the only ones who had accomplished what they had come to do. Henry had his Mena and would certainly take her and the girl back with him. Wayne had found a lost island and a lot to add to his book, although it didn't quite meet the title. The bishop had not yet saved a single soul. Adam had no particular objective and, for that reason, did not know if he had accomplished anything.

On the way back, the bishop's thoughts were still with the gods, whom he could have touched if he had walked a little further. His God was, oh, so far away. The locals here didn't really have to quietly pray to their god as they did. They could almost holler.

CHAPTER 7

A few days passed uneventfully. It's amazing how quickly people can adjust to the proverbial "sweet doing nothing", sitting under waving palm trees, with the ocean slowly licking the sandy beach in front of them. No wonder "going to the island" is proverbial for total relaxation. This place was even all inclusive, no booze, though.

Henry had moved out of the hospital hut and into Mena's. She had so many questions about the place, where he had been. Piece by piece he told her, and noticed how her original astonishment turned into fear, although he made it really easy for her to comprehend.

"We always knew," he said, "that our island wasn't all there is, and really, there's much, much more. More people, too. But, in essence, it is like here. People live on land, not on the water, just like us. If they all stayed in the place where they were born, there wouldn't be any difference at all. However, they are restless, always wanting to go to other places. When they go on the water, it's still, like here. Their canoes are bigger; that's all. Only, if they go over land, then it's different. They travel in vehicles not unlike canoes, but closed in; they roll over land at high speeds on broad trails.

There is one other way, how they move from place to place: they can fly. That's something we cannot do, but we see it all around us. The birds and the insects fly from one place to the other. Then they sit down and are again on land like we are." Henry stopped there, because he noticed Mena was getting dizzy even from his very basic description of the outside world. She had to be prepared, though, for when he took her there, and that would be very soon.

Another time, he therefore, continued his explanation of civilization. “As I said, there are many more people. They all want a place on land. Pretty much all space in a desired area is taken up by houses, the equivalent to our huts. When there is no more space, they build their houses on top of each other.”

“That’s impossible; they crash.”

“No, they don’t. The walls are made of very sturdy material. Just picture a tree trunk. A tree holds a lot of weight and high up into the air. Their huts are like tree houses, but with somebody living underneath.

“Now, when all these people living on higher floors all come down and gather in front of the ground floor hut, there is hardly any space to stand. It’s so crowded. When they do their favorite pastime, which is moving, that’s called traffic, and it takes some time to get used to.”

Sometimes Henry went out with the fishermen. His white friends then saw him only at the distribution. That, of course, meant no more translator. All three of them knew by now how to say “yes” and “no” and “thank you” in the local language.

But that was it. A language with no writing is so much harder to learn than one written down and preferably in the familiar Arabic letters.

The bishop nodded off frequently, but when he was awake, he still thought about how to win the locals for Christianity. Henry, his translator, was busy and after his confession, to have his own personal god, he would not have been a good assistant, anyway. Believing in a personal god was not something the bishop could tolerate. The whole church organization, including himself, would not be necessary anymore in such a scenario.

Maybe Adam had an idea. The bishop turned to him. “Adam, you read all these books, you know, the ones in our church library that nobody ever takes out. You must have come across stories of missionaries in foreign countries with a different language, where nobody understood them. How did they do it?”

“Most of them with a translator. Some learned the local language, but even that is easier with a translator or at least a dictionary, something in print with both languages on it. In many cases, the king, or whoever was in power, decided it by decree and everybody was Christian overnight. Some missionaries, like St. Francis Xavier, the most successful missionary of all times, concentrated on baptism. Anybody baptized would go to heaven, no matter what else they believed in. He is said to have baptized 100, 000 people in Asia, whereby he didn't shy away from force, if somebody didn't want to be."

"Enough, enough," interrupted the bishop. "I've heard about cruelties, but most stories are overdone, I'm sure. There are black sheep in every flock. We both know that."

"Yes, I do know that, but Xavier is now a saint. His baptizing arm is a relic in Rome. It hasn't decomposed, not in four hundred years. Makes you think."

For a while, both men were deep in thought, or did they succumb to the midday heat? It was Adam who picked up the conversation again. "I once read a book about a missionary being sent to a small island, palm trees and all, not unlike here. I think what I read there comes closest to your situation. When he got there, he didn't speak the language, either, but he learned it. Took him two years, though."

"How did he gain the trust of the locals before he could talk to them in their language?"

"I'm not sure, but I think he healed a small boy, who basically was given up by everybody, including his father. To the locals, any of our regular medicines, when it worked, would appear to be a sign of unbelievable power by the Christian god."

The bishop had not yet paid much attention to the medicine man, but he had noticed that healing was about eighty percent of what this man did. He was more like a physician than a spiritual leader. He would in all likelihood not look kindly at any healing done by the bishop.

The medicine man ranked quite high in this society, just like a physician does in civilized countries. The ranking was something that bothered the bishop more and more. He was used to being the crème de la crème in his hometown. There was the physician, like here, but also the school principal, the mayor, and the pharmacist. And, of course, himself, the priest. He considered himself to be the alpha guy in this society, because he had God's backing. None of the others did. On this island, the master seemed to be highest ranking, higher than the medicine man. He would, therefore, be his equal, but he had not seen the master since they had arrived. No invitation, no little chat among leaders. The bishop was quite unhappy but didn't know how to correct the situation.

A little bit farther down the beach, Wayne was obviously not bothered by anything. He and Rona had found a liking to each other. Right then, they were playing in the shallow water like kids, or was it lovers? Rona pretended to escape on land, but Wayne caught her again and again and carried her into deeper water and dropped her there. Rona could, of course, swim like a fish. Everybody here did. Contrary to the bishop, Wayne didn't need much knowledge of the language to play that game, but he was, in fact, way ahead of the other two whites in learning it. As it's been said, there is no better way to learn a foreign language than having a lover who speaks it.

CHAPTER 8

The following day was a holiday. It felt to the whites like a Sunday, but it was celebrated in honour of the moon. With no stark contrasting seasons like winter and summer, the people had only the moon to measure the passage of time. There were twenty-nine nights between two full moons. The return of the full moon was definitely a good reason for celebration. In a more practical way, in the absence of artificial light, the bright moon provided light enough to celebrate late into the night.

Most islanders dressed up a little. They put on their finest tapa skirts, those decorated with colorful bird feathers or fresh flowers, and so on. Some women were wearing bracelets or chains with pretty attachments. Rona looked very attractive and Wayne adored her. Something in her chain caught his eye. It looked like some white pebbles that reflected the moonlight.

Wayne had a closer look at the necklace, slowly turning it around Rona's neck along her breasts. Rona found that not to be a bad start for the evening. She was disappointed, then, when she was asked to take the necklace off and to hand it to him. He looked at it, felt the smoothness of the white objects. These are pearls, he concluded; these are really and surely quite valuable pearls.

He didn't know much about pearls, just what everybody learns in school. They grow in various kinds of oysters. Whenever some foreign object gets into the oyster, the animal grows a mucous around that sand corn or whatever caused the irritation. The developing pearl grows from the same material as the oyster shell, but is smoother and, therefore, shinier.

It didn't come as a complete surprise to Wayne that the islanders had pearls. After all, he had seen shells on the beach. The people picked them up, checked if they were still good to eat and would notice the pearls if there were any. Most were open and dead, and were no longer good for eating. How many could there be? The islanders had been here for three generations. If they only found ten a year, that would add up to a few nice strands.

Wayne asked Rona to give him the chain, assuring her that he would return it. He raised his hand to swear, but Rona somehow misunderstood the gesture. She got up, gave him the chain and left. So much for a romantic evening. Henry told Wayne later on that the meaning of this gesture with the hand was very close to a well-known hand gesture in the western world. That evening, though, Wayne had only one thought: how to lay his hands on these pearls. Not just Rona's. He saw pearls everywhere now, around necks and wrists, even ankles. They must be worth a fortune. What would he do as a millionaire, what would his brother Bill say, what, the neighborhood? Wayne left the party to be alone under the stars and started dreaming.

All kinds of traditional games and dances were going on. A lot of them included some burning sticks that were thrown up into the air and expertly caught when they came down. There was fire all along the beach. With so much driftwood collecting at the edge of the water, there was no lack of fuel. Some young men moved the burning wood away from one of the fireplaces and then, one after the other, walked barefoot over the glowing coals. None of them suffered serious burns on their soles. A miracle, attributed to their personal god and protector. Then it was Henry's turn and, surprisingly, he could do it, too.

Next, the crowd pointed out Adam and the bishop. Adam refused, but the bishop figured, his god was just as strong or more so. He badly burned his feet. They looked for Wayne, but he was nowhere to be seen.

Henry and Mena were quietly sitting in the warm sand, deep in thought. They knew the whites would not stay forever. The master's plan to take away the boat was, of course, unknown to them. Henry thought it as a given that Mena and

Reila would come with him, to live in the town, where he was now used to living.

It was beautiful to sit there by the ocean in the moonlight, but Henry wanted to leave as soon as possible. He more and more missed the spoils of civilization. Thoughts like what would he do if his pants tore? Would he go back to a skirt? He mentally went through all his clothes, and it was basically the same with all of them. Nothing would last forever. Never to read a book or watch TV, or not knowing what was going on in the world, bothered him. He almost panicked when he thought of Reila getting sick, with just an ordinary open wound and no antiseptics, or having an infection without antibiotics.

Mena understood; the medical situation would be much better in a civilized country; the way Henry had explained civilization. Would there be a strong medication against homesickness? Really bad homesickness, as she would have it for sure.

Thinking of medicine, there was the medicine man, too. Everybody was there. He sat down close to the bishop. Henry had told him what the bishop's function was in his own world. The two could not converse directly.

The medicine man pointed to the bishop's feet. The bishop let him have a look. The other man shook his head, obviously, an international gesture. Then he left but soon came back with a coconut shell full of some green paste. He looked to the bishop, silently asking if he should put it on. The bishop nodded furiously. "What the hell, pardon heaven, let him put it on. It can't get worse." The medicine man did, and fifteen minutes later the worst pain was gone. Should the bishop acknowledge that? To his credit, he did. He shook the "doctor's" hand, and that's how the two became tentative friends.

Later in the evening, one of the young fellows fell from a horizontal pole during a hairy balancing act. He badly hit his head and seemed to have quite a headache. The medicine man went up from where he was sitting and had a look. Obviously, there was nothing he could do to help. The bishop took two Aspirin out of his pocket. He always had them with him because of his occasional migraines. The young lad swallowed them and soon claimed he was better. Both pseudo doctors smiled.

CHAPTER 9

It was his new friend, the medicine man, who gestured to the bishop the following day, indicating to follow him. Up the trail to the master's house they went. The bishop wondered why Henry was not the one taking him. With him, there would be a translator present and a conversation with the master possible, without him, not.

The bishop didn't only want to understand what the master wanted from him; he had some important questions, too. For instance, why they, the islanders, were hiding from the rest of the world. In fact, he might have to tell him about the rest of the world and where it was and what it looked like. And then, of course, the bishop's main objective: to start converting the population to Christianity. Would the master help him?

Once there, the medicine man turned around and went back. The door to the master's house was opened by a young lad. "Come in," he said.

It took a moment before the bishop realized that he spoke English, English as clear as it gets. He was relieved to have a translator after all. The conversation with the master had a much better chance of going smoothly and have results. Now he had even more questions for the master, and he could ask them all.

The young fellow led him into a big room, nicely decorated but still in the style of a hut, which itself was part of a small village.

The lad left, and the master pointed for the bishop to sit down on a wooden bench with lots of comfortable cushions. No indication yet whether he also spoke English. After a few sips from a coconut drink, the master started a long monologue about the history of the island. Yes, he did speak English, and it was good, except for a few mispronounced letters and sometimes the emphasis on the wrong syllable.

"Two generations ago, my grandfather, with my then young grandmother, was sent as missionary to an island not too far from here. The name of the place was Koruk, which simply meant "home." The island we are on now is also called that. The missionary's work made slow progress, but after about five years of hard work, the population had been completely baptized.

Another village was on the other side of this island. The two had not much contact with each other. One reason was a rough and mountainous center of the island, which was difficult to cross. Another might have been the fact, the missionaries in this other village were of a different denomination. The two missionaries were not hostile to each other but did not promote contact between their flocks because of fear, of losing some to the other side."

The master paused for a moment, giving the bishop a chance to form a picture in his mind of another island with lush, green vegetation, surrounded by blue ocean. A nice place to be.

"Then, one hot day, dark clouds were moving in. Soon the sunlight was disappearing in the middle of the day. And then the wind picked up, and how it did. Within an hour, almost the whole island was blown away. No trees were standing; the crop in the field was blown into the ocean. This strongest cyclone anybody could remember even blew some top soil away."

Once the bishop had adjusted the imaginary sunny island in his mind to the harsh reality, he was glad to not be there.

The master continued to further destroy the bishop's vision, "The result was, among other things, a tremendous shortage of food for the surviving people. They were starving. No help was in sight. The surrounding islands and the adjacent mainland had sustained major damage. Ships with food and other materials would certainly come, but at the time, without communication, there was no way of knowing when.

My grandfather must have had an excellent talent for organization and a clear foresight. He had the people in his village collect all food that was still there. He divided it into daily rations for one month and handed it out accordingly. Our free food distribution is still based on this event."

"What about the other village?" The bishop was thinking and got his answer right away.

"In the other village, the entire missionary team had been killed in the storm, but the chief did the same as my ancestor. After a few days, however, the food storage was stormed by the mob, all food eaten, a lot of it even spoiled in the ensuing fights. People were dying of hunger and of sickness, because of contaminated wells. The people in this other village had absolutely nothing to eat or drink.

They had no boats anymore, either, to come over and get some food from my grandfather's place. Their boats had been blown into the ocean or shattered against trees during the storm.

Sensing that, my grandfather's village sent two canoes with basic food over, but the situation was so bad there, the villagers attacked the relief mission before they could come on land. The paddlers had to dump everything into the shallow water close to the beach."

The bishop added a few corpses to his imaginary island. Mostly, though, he wondered how the master would ever get to what really interested him, this island, the one they were on and its population.

“Next day, some of the unfriendly villagers were seen in my grandfather’s place. They had come over the mountains, something nobody had done in many years. Obviously, the storm had blown some trails into the dense vegetation, which had appeared to be impenetrable before. These refugees got some food—it was the Christian thing to do.

However, they also brought their slightly different understanding of Christianity with them, one my grandfather could not accept. Church services became difficult. He tried to reconcile the two views of Jesus’s life but made little progress. Old wounds broke open again, from the time, not long ago, when the two villages were permanently at war and raided each other.”

The bishop knew of the previous constant warfare among the various island nations. In fact, many people regarded the newly established peace as the most important missionary accomplishment. In their eyes, saving the souls was a by-product. The bishop saw it the other way around, of course.

The master continued, "Then an unknown family, parents with four children, arrived. They were fleeing a big war farther north. Everybody knew, there was a war. Warplanes were often seen high overhead. Once, a warship was seen in the distance. A big one, much bigger than the government's island shuttle and bigger than any ship the natives had ever built.

The strangers in their canoe had not been directly involved in the war, but once, not too long ago, two of these high-flying aircraft had left their formation and had come down, shooting at the people in their village. Nobody was hit, but this family had decided not to be part of target practice ever again."

The bishop wondered whether these had been Japanese or American planes. Maybe they had been Australian. Too late to find out. The people having seen them were no longer here.

The master suspected, those planes occasionally seen overhead might be warplanes, not transport for the gods as it was commonly believed. It did not matter as long as everybody looked for cover not to be seen when one could be heard.

Finally, the master was getting to the point. "Taking all these adversities into account, my grandfather suggested to the elders of the village to move south, where there was more food and less war activity. They agreed. Moving from island to island was in their blood. That's how they got here."

The bishop noticed the master was an excellent storyteller and would have delivered outstanding sermons, but he didn't, and that was the point.

"Now, two generations later, hunger is gone, but the fear of dying from starvation is still present. That's why we keep the population at a number the land can support. That is about ninety persons, and we avoid being detected by the outside world and getting drawn into another war. We are content. Even better, we feel we are in paradise here on earth."

At this point, the bishop had to interrupt. "You are descendants of missionaries. Why is it, then, that the people here are not Christians in the generally accepted sense? Most of them pray to their own god."

"Good question. They still were real believers, as long as my grandfather lived. But keeping the faith was hard for them. After all, my ancestor's god had, first of all, not prevented the hurricane, and then he let his people starve to death. During the following generation, slowly but surely, they modified their Christian belief. It's still one god but a personal one, more like a guardian angel, in addition to Christ, not replacing him."

"I don't think so," the bishop interrupted. "When I listen to the people praying, I never hear the words Jesus or Christ."

"Well, it's true," admitted the master. "Some merge the guardian angels with their ancestors and put Jesus on the back seat."

"Wouldn't that be the old ancestor worship, no Christ at all?"

"Yes and no. We live a Christian life. The food distribution, the hospital, the daycare and the soup kitchen, they all go back to the former mission. We also brought skills here, like how to make pottery, to make tools from wood and stone. Luckily, we still have some metal tools like knives and axes, which they brought here and we would not be able to produce ourselves."

The bishop decided not to pursue the subject of Jesus Christ versus individual ancestor gods any further. At least not now. He knew of the Mexican night of the dead celebrations, when people visit the graves of their ancestors and bring them food and other presents. They celebrate together and pretend to be the happy and complete family they once were, while the ancestors were still alive.

When the bishop first heard of this custom, he figured these people must be heathens. But then he realized, they were not. Instead, they were very Catholic. Mexico is one of the most Catholic nations on earth. The people's Catholic faith doesn't seem to interfere with the old custom or vice versa.

Many years ago, the bishop himself was wondering why dead ancestors could not help the living. After all, they were in heaven, close to God and had his ear, so to speak. After a while, he pushed these thoughts away. Ancestor worship and a regulated church of any kind just don't mix.

The bishop turned the discussion to another surprise. "Why is it that you speak English and some of your family members do, too?"

"We are all descendants of the missionary, my grandfather. We do not only speak and teach our kids English, we are real Christians, with one god, to whom we pray. We don't dare to show it, though, because there are some radical elements in our society. The medicine man has been waiting ever since he took over from his father, to split the population and to move in here as new master. Then there is the growing group of non-believers. Holding the village together is our main objective now; religion comes second."

The master made it quite clear that he felt uncomfortable. The bishop let him off the hook for now.

CHAPTER 10

The two men sat there in silence until the bishop asked another one of the many questions he had. "How come you are the master and your family is, in effect, running the place?"

"It's a combination of things. Nobody is alive anymore who witnessed that exodus from our previous home, but everybody knows that our family saved them and most are still grateful.

Secondly, we are whites, and white skin is something strongly associated with superiority by all indigenous peoples. Their first contact with Europeans was with soldiers, traders, farmers and, yes, missionaries, and they all were white and were accepted by the locals as superior, although, quite often, their land was taken away or they were forced to work for the newcomers as slaves. Many died in the process."

The bishop had heard of the intense discussions between the leaders at the time of his own church, as to whether the natives would be humans or not. For a while, they were treated accordingly.

"Based on these experiences, there seems to be an idiotic and absolutely unjustified subconscious ranking by skin color in the world," the master continued his lecture, "whereby light-colored is highest ranking and black is lowest. Our people here are somewhere in the middle. They are, in fact, a bit darker than the average, my grandfather always said. I don't have a comparison. As a matter of fact, Adam's skin, after all his sunbathing, is now just as dark as most people's here."

The bishop agreed. "I remember when my dad told me stories about the outside world; he referred to the natives of America as red skins.

In the pictures of the books he read from, they weren't red at all, just sometimes painted red on their faces, but the color stuck. Chinese people are sometimes referred to as yellow. That would put them below white but ahead of American Indians."

The bishop was about to say the suppression of non-Caucasian people was luckily coming to an end. It wasn't quite as bad anymore, as the master saw it. But then he remembered, the master's view of the world was based on what his father had told him many years ago. With no contact with the outside world, he could not know any better. Neither could the villagers, who were still accepting the old hierarchy by skin colour.

"But is that really all it takes to establish leadership?" The bishop was thinking of his flock at home and how he had to fight, to stay on top. Most of them, of course, had all the same color as his skin—white.

"Not quite," the master continued. "You have to offer your people something they wouldn't have without you. For instance," he elaborated, "after the completely unexpected horrific disaster by the hurricane, my grandfather started to record the weather. His son, my father, continued, and

I'm still doing it. There hasn't been such a strong hurricane since, but there have been many rough seas. When I sense there's one coming, and I see the pattern from up here, I blow the trombone, which my ancestor saved and brought here, and the fishermen come quickly home. That service is very much appreciated. They might think I have the information from my powerful God; that's at least what I hope. Without God's support, real or just perceived, there is no leadership."

The master wasn't finished yet. "Here is another example, more down to earth. I see many petty crimes from up here with my scope, brought here by my grandfather. With it, I often see when somebody is misbehaving down at the beach or in the village. The people here are always shocked when I know these things at the court sessions. If that's not superiority, what is?"

"You've been born here. You have never seen a car, have never listened to radio or watched TV." The bishop went quickly through the mathematics to guess when the master was born, probably around 1950. The subject of these mathematics shrugged.

"Did I miss much?" The young lad came in again with some lunch.

"My youngest son," the master introduced. The lunch consisted of boiled eggs, sweet potatoes, mangoes, breadfruit and coco milk, again, all nicely decorated on banana leaves and the all-purpose coconut shell.

"You are certainly not starving anymore," the bishop remarked.

"No, and we have quite a food storage, with which we can help out our supporters occasionally."

"I guess, when you need supporters, you also have enemies. Is that so?"

"Unfortunately, yes, we do. The medicine man has tried for many years to take over from me as master. "

"How would he do that? You seem to have everything under control."

"Yes and no," was the master's answer. "He is the one behind the variations of Christianity. He can be quite flexible, supporting whatever the people believe. I can't, I have to stick to God's word in the Bible."

The master changed the subject. He wanted to get back to skin colour. "As I said earlier, our main advantage, which nobody can take away, is our skin, combined with our supernatural abilities, which the locals see as result of a close connection to God, our strong God."

"Some members of my family can write and pass on messages to each other. That's being seen as pure magic by the villagers."

The bishop was deep in thought: Written communication was a major factor in religion, positive or negative. His Catholic church's monopoly of God was pretty much lost, after the parishioners could read the Bible just as the priest did. When he now said something not in the Bible, they noticed it.

"There is one problem with our superiority," the master said, noticeably reluctant to bring up the subject of skin color again, after the lad had taken away what lunch was left, "We are running out of white skin. My grandparents were white. Their two sons were, too, of course. One of them, my father, married his long-term fiancée from home:, that's my mother, but the other married a local girl. Both marriages produced children, two white boys including myself and three mixed race girls on my uncle's side."

The master paused for a moment. The story moved more and more into the very personal and private realm, and he knew even more private matters were still to come.

"We are thirteen people up here, all related," the master said. "Six of them are old enough to get married and produce the next generation in order to ensure our continued existence. The children out of these unions will be very cute, I'm sure, but rather dark-colored with Polynesian or Melanesian features. I've already made plans about how we could survive as regular members of the nation, but it's unlikely it'll work. Whenever somebody comes down from a higher level, he or she gets hammered as revenge. Just think of the outcome of all these revolutions in history, like the French revolution in the late seventeen hundreds and many more that followed, up to our time."

"What can I do?" the bishop asked. He was ready to help out, as Christian to Christian and because the two men were in a similar leadership role. But he didn't trust his ears when he listened to the master's preposition.

"If you three whites stay here for a while and meet with three of the girls, I mean, if you create children, relatively white children, we could continue the present relationship with the natives for at least the next generation. My family would provide you with everything you need. We build you a home, make sure you have always enough food, and, of course, your wives would bring up the children as is the custom here, no obligation for you whatsoever."

Without having to ponder this proposition, the bishop answered spontaneously, "You have to count me out. I'm an ordained priest and my family is the trinity. I swore to celibacy and I intend to keep my promise to God. As for the other two, I will ask them and if any of them is willing, they will come to you. I don't want to be involved any further in matchmaking or, rather, breeding arrangements."

The master was certainly disappointed, although there were two white young men still left. Maybe he could convince them to participate. As for the bishop, the master made one last attempt. "You know," he said, "you wouldn't really have to marry one of the girls. Your sperm to refresh our gene pool is all we need. We would take care of the rest."

The bishop was disgusted just thinking of sleeping with a girl.

The master, however, had no idea how the bishop felt and misinterpreted the bishop's silence.

"Don't you sometimes think of sex, at night, when you are all alone? I mean, sex is part of being human. Our good Lord created us that way. He shouldn't now blame us for exercising it. Come on. It's so easy to trigger a little sperm to flow."

The bishop knew all about it and had been fighting it all his life. But he didn't want to talk anymore about the subject. This time, a very attractive young girl saw him out. Maybe she was a prime candidate.

CHAPTER 11

Back in their hospital hut, the bishop looked for the other two whites. Only Adam was there; Wayne was with Henry in the villages to buy pearls. How to do that, Wayne didn't quite know, but he hoped to learn it from Henry. He had some money with him, but he knew by then that it was worthless on this island. The villagers didn't know money. They didn't need it. There was nothing to buy. Every family had about the same basic items and they were sufficient: a wooden table, a few mats to sit on, grass mattresses for every family member, two or three clay or metal pots, lots of coconut shells as cups, and banana leaves and trunks as plates. That was it.

Henry became used to money and purchases during his time at the bishop's place. The bishop had given him pocket money, mostly to buy ice cream, his favorite. Cloth and everything else he needed was given to him by church members. Food was provided at the bishop's household. In the early days, Henry had just pointed at the flavor of ice cream in the store and he got some. Everybody knew he was the bishop's new kid. But after a while, the clerk wanted payment. Henry told the bishop about this odd behavior and got a quick lesson in economics, but also regular pocket money from then on.

Now it was the other way around. Henry had to explain to Wayne once more the giving culture of the islanders. "You just point at something," he said, "and it is given to you." All three whites were by now used to having their space in the hut and their food given to them without charge. But buying pearls, luxury items, for nothing, brought this custom to an extreme.

The system did work, though. Henry took Wayne to the first house in the first village. He introduced Wayne and both men were welcomed in a very polite and warm way. Wayne noticed it was obviously bad manners to announce the reason for the visit too soon. First Henry had to show his interest in the well-being of the visited family. He was offered a coconut with coco milk and the islander's favorite food, a banana. Wayne made a quick calculation and figured, at that speed, he would have to stay at least a month to visit every house.

Eventually, Henry turned the conversation to pearls. Would the lady of the house have any? And yes, she did. "Would she mind giving some to Wayne, as a souvenir, when he went back to his land? He can't carry much in the small boat, because we must face the strong current surrounding the island. Pearls are lightweight and don't take up much space. They also don't dissolve when they get wet and they would be, for sure, in the rough seas."

The lady gave Wayne six of her eighteen pearls. The others, she wanted to keep for her three-year-old girl to play with. Wayne almost flipped out. Hundreds of dollars were being played with in the sand. The choking hazard did not even come to mind as it is the case with all hazards in pursuit of wealth.

The next hut didn't have any, but the third one had a lot of them, all rolling on the floor, most covered with sand. Wayne went down on his knees and started picking them up. "You can't do that," whispered Henry in English. "They have to be given to you, with a smile and a bow, like in the first house. What you did looks like you are cleaning the floor, and that is the wife's job." Not all was lost, though. The lady asked them to come back tomorrow, after she had done her housework, including cleaning the floor.

And so it went in this first village. Some visits were successful, others not. For Henry, it was a chance to meet the neighbors again, whom he hadn't seen in two years. There were new babies to admire and compliments of all sorts to be exchanged. Everybody, pearls or not, saw the whole tour as a polite introduction of Wayne to the community. "Thanks, Henry, for introducing the white man. We have never seen one before."

Wayne carried the pearls in a coconut shell. Everything small enough was carried that way. In the last house of the village, Henry and Wayne did their usual dance, asking about everybody's health and the husband's outlook on fishing. Yes, fish were plentiful, enough to dry some for meager days. And how was Reila?

Before Henry could start the subject of pearls, the lady of the house saw Wayne's collection of pearls in the coconut shell. "Oh," she cried out, "just what I need to finish my waistband." She fetched it from some corner of the hut and showed the guests the unfinished work with lots of pearls but with some still missing. "You have to give her all your pearls—it's expected," said Henry, in English again.

Near dark, Henry went home to his family while Wayne, a very much frustrated Wayne, went to the hospital, where the whites were staying. The bishop had waited for the crew to be complete and once it was, he told his boys what had happened at the master's house, everything about the English they spoke, the history of the island, and the white skin. He stopped short of mentioning the subject of marriage or sperm. That, he wanted to elaborate on as a separate issue. He was looking forward to their reaction. It would be very interesting, because these two men could not be more different in their views.

"So, they have a two-tier society," said Adam after a while. "The rich, white people up on the hill and the poor, dark devils in the jungle. It's really not a surprise. Also, did you notice, we always eat before the women and how they only get our leftovers when they sit down? Sometimes, we don't leave them anything, and they accept it. That would actually make it a three-tier society, the whites, the black men, and the women."

"It's a macho world pretty much everywhere," added the bishop, "except for the so-called western world, and even there it has started to change only in the last few years." The bishop forgot that the Catholic church has been a man's world for two thousand years with no improvement in sight.

Wayne saw it differently. "I had a look into several huts today. The people there seem to be quite content, happy even."

"That's the problem," Adam countered. "The lower classes often don't even realize they are suppressed."

The discussion went on for quite some time. In the end, the bishop and Wayne agreed: there was a not justifiable difference between the circumstances up on the hill and the people down here, but not as dramatic as in the western world where about one percent of the population owns about fifty percent of the world's assets. Adam still felt something had to be done to advance life on the island to true equality.

Time for the bishop to bring up the real tricky subject of gene pool improvement up on that hill. That sure got the boys' attention. Wayne was eager to find out the practicalities. Would the girls come down here? They only had one room. Or would the whites spend a night in the master's quarters? Which of the girls would he get, and would there be a choice? His problem with getting the pearls, which had occupied his thoughts all evening, was suddenly a minor issue.

Adam ruined it all by saying, "I won't do it."

"Why not?" Wayne didn't understand Adam's immediate reaction. "That's a unique opportunity to combine a good deed with pleasure."

"I don't want my son or daughter to grow up in this primitive environment. After all, any child would be my flesh and blood, part of me. I would not even know how my child is doing. I would not be able to come here again and to help out like parents do everywhere. I don't even have to think long about it. A friend of mine from the youth group, a student, is a sperm donor. He suggested I do it too, to get some pocket money. I said no for the same reasons."

Wayne was looking for support. "How about you, bishop?"

"I can't," the bishop said.

"You are not castrated, or are you?"

Adam could have told him he wasn't.

"I won't tell anybody back home what you did here," Wayne tried again. "Is it not an obligation for a Christian minister to help his sheep in an emergency? The prevention of inbreeding is one."

"It's getting late." The bishop didn't want to discuss his own relationship to sperm any further. "Looks like you are the only candidate, Wayne. Talk to the master tomorrow and hear what he says."

When Henry came home that same evening after the pearl shopping spree, he told Mena about all he had learned from the neighbors and how Wayne started out with no pearls and also finished that way. It took him a while to notice.

She sat there, stone-faced, not showing any interest. She had gone through Henry's backpack and had found the glossy photo book of Auckland, which Henry intended to show her, but hadn't been brave enough yet. She had seen the immense crowd moving up and down Queen street, and the huge sky tower, higher than ten palm trees on top of each other, and the busy harbor. Maybe Henry had not lied to her, but he had given her a lousy description of civilization. She had decided she didn't want any part of it.

CHAPTER 12

Wayne didn't sleep much that night, thinking about the details of his duty. He checked his equipment and found it in good working order. He got up before breakfast and walked up the hill towards the master's quarters to discuss with him how he could help. When he came close enough to be seen, a young man came out of one of the huts. He asked Wayne whom he wanted to see up there and whether he had an appointment. He did that in perfect English, but that didn't surprise Wayne anymore.

The quick answer going through Wayne's mind was: I'm here to sleep with your sister or cousin. That would have been not only impolite but outright dangerous. The young man was dressed in the customary skirt, not much else, letting his mighty muscles show. It was clear to Wayne: this was not your friendly receptionist; this was a bodyguard.

What he really answered was, "I'm here to discuss with the master the issue of gene pool."

Hard to say if that rang a bell in the bodyguard's mind. He answered, "Wait here. Let me see if the master is available." As soon as he disappeared into one of the huts, another young man came out and joined the waiting Wayne.

This security arrangement reminded Wayne of an instance in his cab-driving life. He was asked to bring a small parcel to an ex-minister, now chairman of the board of an arms manufacturer and to hand it over personally. There, he was checked three times by men who looked like bodyguards. The last station, however, was a very attractive young secretary. When he saw her, he knew he was close to the minister.

Thinking of that good-looking secretary reminded him of the reason he was here. Yes, the master was available. The first bodyguard took him into the inner sanctum. Well, it was the biggest and nicest hut Wayne had ever seen. The master welcomed him with a smile and a handshake, something not customary on the island, but it seemed to be very appropriate for the close relationship they were planning to have.

A long table had been set for breakfast. The master asked Wayne if he had had something to eat. Wayne wasn't really hungry. He was much too nervous to eat, but it was obvious, nothing would be done or even talked about before breakfast. All members of the family came in now and sat down at the table.

Wayne scanned all the younger women and they, of course, taxed him, all of them, not knowing whether they would be selected or not. The conversation was in the local language, with only periodically a sentence in English. To sit there quietly, not being involved in the lively conversation, made Wayne even more nervous.

With breakfast finished and all others gone, the master brought a piece of very thin wood from somewhere outside and leaned it upright against the wall. Lines and names were scratched upon it. Some lines ended at a name, some continued. The whole thing reminded Wayne of roads on a map, as he had studied them for his taxi exam.

It was, in fact, a genealogy drawing, which the master was looking at from different angles. Then he was saying, more to himself than to Wayne, "When I hoped all three of you would help us out, I had three of our young ladies in mind. Now it's only one. So, who do I pick for you? You will definitely help to improve our gene pool, one way or another, but what helps us best is your skin tone. If I go too dark for the girl, your white may get lost. If I pick a lighter skinned girl, there might not be an overall improvement. I'm white myself, my two sons are rather white, but the girls are all somewhere in-between."

Eventually, the master seemed to have made his decision. He took the board outside again. When he came back, he had a bottle in his hands. A bottle made of clay but, nevertheless, unmistakably in the shape of a bottle. "Have a drink from our banana liquor. That will help you to loosen up. We reserve it for special occasions, and today is one."

The two men chatted about this and that, Wayne rather absent-mindedly, when the side door opened and a woman's voice said, "We are ready."

The master went ahead, and through the door Wayne followed. He didn't trust his eyes when he was inside. There was a woman, stark naked, on her back on a mattress. Around her stood about half a dozen other women. Some talked to the sacrificial lamb, obviously to calm her. One asked her to lift her bum and put a pillow underneath. Then they, one after the other, looked expectantly at Wayne.

He stood there, frozen, unable to move. Unable—that was the word for everything. For a little while, he thought, those ladies would now do to him what they had done to the girl. But they didn't. Maybe they were not familiar with his European clothes. Maybe they just didn't dare touch him. They left the decision of what to do to the only other man in the room, the master.

He grabbed Wayne by the arm and pulled him back into the breakfast room. "I told them, that won't work, but they didn't listen. Come back at nightfall into this hut." He pointed at one in the back of the complex. "The girl will be there. Spend the night with her, and everything will be all right."

CHAPTER 13

When Wayne came back from the hill, the bishop and Adam had finished breakfast but were still sitting at the breakfast table. Wayne's breakfast was there untouched, since he was still expected. The sick or old women had arrived already, but very little was left for them. The weather had been bad and the fishermen were fighting their way back. Half of them had not yet made it back to distribution.

Wayne seemed to be very generous by moving his breakfast over to the women. Adam admired him for his social conscience and said so. Wayne obviously felt uncomfortable getting credit for something he didn't deserve. "I had breakfast earlier, up at the master's."

The bishop and Adam thought they had a pretty good idea of what had happened this morning up on the hill, but they were wrong.

Finally, the rest of the fishing boats came in, Henry among them. Some of the fishermen were quite upset with the master. He hadn't blown his trombone to warn them of the upcoming storm. "That," they were saying, "is the minimum he can do. We do everything else. We should not bring him any fish today." But in the end, they did. Wayne knew what had distracted the master from watching the weather this morning.

From that mild protest, Adam concluded that the master did not have a hundred percent approval rating, as they would have called it at home. "So," Adam said, turning to Henry, "some people seem to be unhappy with the master.

When did you elect him and when does his term end?"

"No, no," Henry laughed. "It's not like that. I know how you elect your presidents or prime minister. I learned that in school, but here it's not like that. It's more like the monarchy in England and other countries. The master inherited it from his father and he from his father, and so on. He has been master as long as I can remember."

Adam slowly warmed up to the subject. "Any position of power should be elected. Maybe somebody can do a better job than the present master. You will never know."

Henry thought about it for a moment. "He has no real power; he blows the trombone and that's it, except for the court sessions."

"Don't you realize, the court is his power? He is the government." Henry was still not convinced.

"He has the five chiefs with him in session," he said.

"Okay, that sounds better. They have a vote, then, in the end."

"Not really. The master decides, after getting council from the chiefs."

"I rest my case," was all Adam had to say about such a dictatorship.

So far, the bishop hadn't said anything. Now he was zooming in on the master. "There isn't only the blowing of the trombone this morning, which he didn't. Much worse is, how he neglected to keep the people here believing in the Lord. You say he has all this power, and yet, he let the missionary work of his ancestors slip away."

"Actually, his father did," Henry said, coming to the defence of the master. "We don't talk much about religion. As you know, there were already differences among our ancestors, when they left home. The way I put the story together, from various remarks by the elders, it was like this: the main reason for the exodus was lack of food. It was seen only as a religious dispute later. The refugees that landed here were still starving. Some died from the lack of food. How could the new, foreign god let that happen, no matter what version of him they believed in?"

"We don't know of God's plans, and without knowing his objectives, we can't judge his action or inaction." The bishop felt more and more uncomfortable. Too often did he have to comfort people in his flock at home, whose corn dried up in the field without rain or, much worse, who had lost a child in a car accident.

Henry continued, "Once people don't understand one act of God, they start doubting others. Finally, they begin to doubt the whole existence of God. The lack of support material contributed to the weakening of the Christian faith after the exodus. There wasn't a single Bible saved and none of the glossy pictures that were even more important than written words which only the missionaries could read. Whatever you see as a picture is much more likely to be true than written text."

It was quite obvious, while living in the bishop's house, Henry had given religion a lot of thought. "We villagers are rather simple-minded, and we tend to obey authority. When somebody like the medicine man says the gods are up at the volcano, we believe that. When the master insists there is only one god and he is up in heaven, we believe that, too. What is a person to do with both messages? As you know, some of us lean this way and some the other, and many try to combine both. That's where we seem to be now."

Since nobody else said anything, Henry continued, "When I said simple-minded, I didn't mean irrational or outright dumb. We like things to be logical and matching our own experience. For instance, my ancestors totally believed in the creation story. Man made from dirt mirrors their own environment, where everything miraculously grows out of dirt. With God wanting a son, we have no problem, either. Also, in the absence of a female god, he had to have the son with a human woman. Again, easy to understand. The woman being a virgin is even easier to comprehend. God just wanted to be sure the child was his. But there our understanding ends. How could the son become the father? That's impossible."

Henry had never talked that much before. The bishop couldn't believe what he heard here by his foster son, whom he had instructed over years on the finer points of Christianity, and here he was doubting the basics.

To make matters worse, Adam was completely on Henry's side and went straight to his main interest: the equality of men and women. "Here is another one of these difficult to understand teachings, going back to creation. Why was Eve created out of Adam's rib? Was God out of dirt?" Adam looked at the bishop and continued courageously, "Is this why women are seen as inferior? Dependent on us men and our donation of one of our body parts? Our teacher in school, Ms. Cartwell, thinks so."

Everybody waited for the bishop to respond, but he didn't. He knew one doesn't become a Christian after all these questions have been satisfactorily answered. One becomes a Christian first. That still doesn't answer the questions, but they don't pop up anymore. Faith was more important than logical answers.

Inequality between the sexes was Adam's subject and that's where he took the conversation again. "We should have our meals together with the women," he suggested. "Not only will it give them the same rank, they will also get more food. Remember this morning, if it hadn't been for Wayne's generosity"—he quickly glanced at Wayne— "if it hadn't been for Wayne's early morning exercise, they would have gone without any food."

Wayne got up from the table. There is not much worse than being blamed for a crime one didn't commit. You might as well have done it and reaped the benefits, like having the money from robbing a bank, at least for a little while, before you get caught.

At this point, Wayne would have been ready to cooperate with the master and his plans for future generations on the island. He didn't quite understand, anymore, why he hadn't earlier. What had happened? He was getting a second chance, though, and he was very much looking forward to it. That would be in the evening, a few hours later. In the meantime, it was back to collecting pearls.

CHAPTER 14

Wayne went and got Henry. Mena came with them. Reila was placed in the daycare. They skipped the first village. The people there knew now of Wayne's pearl collecting, although they didn't understand it. Pearls were mostly for kids, sometimes for women, not generally for grown-ups. If the women of the first village were still ready to trade pearls, they would find him, and that would put him into a much better bargaining situation than him going to them.

Nobody was home in the first hut of the second village. Nobody in the second, either. Mena asked some kids who were playing in front of the house. Their mothers were all in the third hut, the one in the middle.

"A meeting," Mena said to Henry. "A village meeting." Mena was puzzled. She normally knew about these things, but this one caught her by surprise.

When they got to that hut, it looked like a garage sale. All six women of the village had their pearls nicely spread out in front of them on tables or tree stumps or whatever was at hand. The number of pearls was quite different from woman to woman. It ranged from just three to twelve. Since it was with women, Mena took over the bargaining. With men, Henry would have done it. That was the custom and this split did support Adam's quest for equality of the sexes, but he wasn't here to see it.

Wayne knew by then the custom of talking about life's important issues first. That was especially true, if one side wanted something from the other, whether it was eggs or pearls. While Henry sat quietly on a tree stump, Wayne counted all the pearls on display. He got to a total of thirty-five. If he sold them for a hundred dollars apiece, it would give him a profit of $3500. That, unfortunately, would not cover the money lost while not driving his cab. Two hundred on average per pearl looked better. The big unknown in this equation was how long they would stay here before he would drive his cab again.

Mena slowly got to the point. Wayne also knew by then that this was a bartering society with the occasional freebee. To take something from six women and not to give any of them anything was rude. Mena was completely on the side of the women and, therefore, not an unbiased judge. “What do you give them?” she asked Wayne. Henry translated and took over from there on.

What did Wayne have? He took out the contents of his trouser pockets. There wasn’t much. A very used handkerchief, a button that he had lost from his jacket and which he intended to sew back on, once he had needle and thread again, a small pocket-knife, a tiny notepad with matching pen, a safety pin, and a single condom. Wayne demonstrated the pocketknife and blew up the condom since its intended purpose was neither known nor needed on the island. They had found other ways, safer ones, since population control was such an important issue. Wayne didn't need it, either. As a matter of fact, it would have been counterproductive.

A woman with six pearls chose the pocket-knife. Henry had explained the previous day, when Wayne lost all pearls, that he had to agree to the suggested trade. It would have been smarter, not to show all his trade items at once. He should have brought them out one after the other and considered the value of every item against the number of pearls. He had just lost his most valuable item for only six pearls, twenty-nine to go.

On it went. Three pearls for the button, also three for the safety pin, five for the handkerchief, six for the notepad. The woman getting it could not write, but she did draw pictures in the sand. Now she could draw on paper, at least for a while. That left the woman with the most pearls, twelve of them and nice ones, too, getting the rather useless balloon. Wayne could see her thinking, deciding what to do. She wanted the pocketknife but hadn't been quick enough.

At this time, an exhausted Adam came running up the trail to this village. "I'm glad I found you," he said to Wayne and Henry, panting heavily. "Our boat is gone, not at the dock anymore. The bishop wants you to come down right away. We have to find it; otherwise, we are stuck here forever."

Adam turned around and went back right away. Henry followed him and Mena joined the two men. She didn't know if the missing boat was good news or bad. If the boat wasn't found, Henry would probably stay. In any case, she had to pick up Reila from the daycare.

Wayne looked longingly at the twelve pearls. Maybe he could do a quick deal, before he joined the others. The owner of the pearls had come to a decision; she took one pearl and handed it to Wayne. That was still a good trade for the condom, but Wayne wanted all twelve. He reached for them, but she covered them up. There was nobody to translate anymore.

Then the woman pulled on his shirt while uncovering the pearls again. No doubt, that was her offer. Eleven pearls for the shirt. Wayne had run out of time; he had to join the others. "Okay." He nodded. "I have two more shirts in my pack." He got the pearls, in his calculation at least eleven hundred and maybe up to twenty-two hundred dollars' worth.

Taking the shirt was not as dumb as it may look. Yes, the people here did not need shirts, but they knew quite well what textiles were and some remnants of former clothing were still around, cloth that the original refugees had worn but which now was in shreds.

The same was true for the pocketknife. All households had at least one knife of some kind or another, most of them very worn, but steel lasted longer than textiles. There were other items in some places, mostly tools, made of steel or other materials, not available on the island. It all depended on what the ancestors brought along. Over time, there were fewer and fewer items, as they were used up, although they were treasured and cared for like family jewels. All in all, Wayne was quite happy with the day's trading. At this time, he did not yet realize, without a boat, these pearls were all toys again.

CHAPTER 15

Shirtless Wayne was soon joining the others down by the docks. They found out the boat had been missing all morning. During breakfast, some fishermen tried to tell the whites something. Henry was not yet back to translate, and so they didn't understand. When Henry arrived with the other latecomers, he obviously didn't notice it. They were all too upset to notice things like a missing boat and were only talking about the master's failure to blow the trombone and how they almost didn't make it back.

Wayne ran up to the master's place to tell him about the boat and to find out whether he knew where it could be. Somehow, he figured, he was the one to go and ask, because of his closer relationship with the people up there. After all, he would become a member of the family and be visiting a few times.

No guard was stopping him this time.

The master saw him running up the trail and somehow misunderstood the visit. He figured Wayne could not wait till nightfall. Understandable but not the proper timing. But no, he hadn't noticed the boat's departure from up there, so he immediately took out his scope and looked all around the beaches as far as he could see. No motor boat in sight, just the canoes.

While Wayne ran down again with the bad news, the master turned to his two sons. "Where did you put it?"

"In the small cave near Rocky Island, where the fishermen never go. The big boat was quite hard to paddle in the darkness and against the strong wind."

"Is it safe there, or could it get away in a storm?"

"No, we put it there in a storm, and if we could do that, it should be all right in future bad weather."

The master was quite happy with the turn of events. Wayne's sperm was just a start; he wanted all three whites to remain on the island. Eventually, all three would help to strengthen the white or almost-white population on the hill and secure the continuation of white supremacy. The two sons were not quite so happy. They saw their influence at stake, but, for now, obeyed their father.

Henry asked all the fisherman if they had seen anything. They hadn't. They were, however, not surprised by the disappearance of the big boat. After all, it was quite a storm this morning. One said, he always wondered, why the boat wasn't better tied to the two palm trees that served as mooring.

For now, the newcomers had to think of a plan B to get home. Was there a plan B? Henry had managed to fight the strong current once before but did not make it to land. He was lucky to have been picked up by a seaworthy ship. And, of course, he was experienced paddling a canoe. None of the others was. And then there were Mena and Reila, without whom Henry would not leave the island.

Henry figured he would certainly miss some of the conveniences of western civilization. Especially medical service. If he had known they would stay there, he would have absolved a first aid course and taken some basic medicine and other medical supplies with him. He would have been the best medicine man the island ever had. But it was too late now. He had with him a few Band-Aids and a vial with Aspirin: that was it.

The bishop saw the situation as God's will. Had God taken the boat away to guide him? He was obviously chosen to start the conversion to real Christianity again. He actually felt quite good about it. Life at home had gotten quite boring. This was the first time, he admitted this to himself, but it was true. There were the three groups of citizens in his town: the true believers, the pretenders, and the atheists. For many years now, he had not been able to convert a single pretender to real faith and definitely no atheist to be a true believer.

Here, on the island, all possibilities were open again; anything could happen. Here was virgin ground, or, even better, the soil had been prepared by the missionaries on the previous island. He would go to work immediately, starting with the master's family. What kind of Christians were they, really? Not Catholics, that was for sure. But did it matter? The way to Christ was no sightseeing trip, where the road often is the goal. To join Christ, the final arrival is everything, the road doesn't matter.

Wayne, always the incurable optimist, was certain they would find a way to get back from there. He realized it would be later than with the boat. He would still collect pearls, but with more time, he could go slow now; he would not give another shirt away so easily.

But something else was bothering Wayne. He didn't know whether he should keep his appointment for the night. Fathering a child as a favour was no problem, but living here to see it born and growing up was a different story all together. At thirty-two years old, he was not yet married, because he was very picky with the ladies. Even when he felt one was good for him, he always tried to imagine what kind of family life they would have, what kind of mother she would be. Here, he did not have any idea what kind of woman he was supposed to sleep with. In other words, tonight's event could turn into not only a blind date but a blind marriage of sorts.

Adam knew, already, what he would do to get away. He was the only one with a real plan B. He would build a catamaran out of two canoes, to be more stable in rough water than a single canoe. He would make a sail out of his cloth. Some canoes here had a sail, but close to shore, when Adam could see them, the fishermen always paddled. He would train for about a week and then simply go. If he drowned, that was still better than living in a dictatorship. Wayne promised to help with building the catamaran but would probably not have much time, since he would collect more pearls and had business up on the hill.

Henry said he would find an experienced canoe builder, but he himself would find it difficult to do more than translating. Like the bishop, he was ready to accept whatever fate had in store. He just didn't call it God's will.

Adam was not at all discouraged; he would build that catamaran, and if the others didn't want to help, he would do it alone. He would, however, not take any passengers who weren't involved in building the boat. Maybe his chances of survival were even better with a lighter load.

The shadows had grown long. The sun would set within a few minutes. Time for Wayne to go to the master's quarters. He had come to a decision. If he really got stuck on the island, having a family here would be better than being alone. If he only knew what kind of woman they had allotted to him. He could not remember what the naked woman looked like. A woman she was, that he was sure of. He could also not be certain the woman tonight would be the one he had been presented with in the morning.

Again, he did not meet a guard on his way up. In fact, he did not see anybody. Several huts were of similar design. What if he picked the wrong one and was intruding in the master's, molesting his wife?

It was pitch dark by now. Wayne went to the entrance of the main house, from where the master had pointed out the smaller hut for tonight's events. Standing on the spot where he stood that morning, he was sure now where he was expected tonight. It was difficult, though, to find the proper entrance in the dark. He was still searching for it and probing the walls when a soft hand touched his arm and gently pulled him inside.

There was no light inside, either. He was completely dependent on his feel of touch. This time she, if it was the same woman, was not naked. She was wearing something, including a top. For a while, the two of them were busy peeling each other. With the boat of the whites away, she was certainly looking for a long-term relationship. And why not? Wayne was a handsome guy. This turned out to be one of the best nights Wayne had ever had. That was definitely true for the woman, because it was her first. Wayne left before morning, without ever seeing his playmate by light.

CHAPTER 16

Next morning, Wayne slept in. Rona did not put his breakfast on the table. She knew he would, in all likelihood, sleep in. Fish doesn't last long out in the sun. She turned her main attention to Adam now. She had noticed how, in fact, Adam was most smitten by her appearance, not Wayne. He was a lost case, but Adam was not so bad after all, she figured. Adam was smaller than Wayne, but he was also much younger. And, of course, she, too, was looking for a longer relationship with a white man after the boat had disappeared and the whites were stuck there.

Adam and the bishop were still sitting at the breakfast table, lately with the sick women, as Adam had insisted. An older man came by looking for Adam. "I build boat," he said in English. Adam was excited to find a boat builder he could talk to. His chances of getting off the island had just gotten much better. Relieved, he explained in some detail what he wanted built, until he realized these were the only three words Henry had taught the man.

Adam drew the outlines of a canoe in the sand. The ship builder, whose name was Taos, understood very well. "Yes, yes, I build boat." He drew another back end of the canoe, which would have made it longer, and then another back line, which would have made it shorter. Quite obviously, he wanted to know the length of it.

So far, so good. Adam looked over to the dock to see how long the canoes of the locals were. They were all the same length. Obviously, the shipbuilders on the island, together with the fishermen, had found out over many years what length provided the optimum stability. That was the length he wanted. He went down to the boats and pointed at all of them, while spreading his arms, indicating length. Taos understood again. That communication without talking turned out to be quite easy.

Then Adam moved two canoes parallel to each other and put two paddles across. Taos seemed to have understood but had his doubts. He had never build a catamaran before since he, too, was born on the island and the ancestors/refugees had not brought one of theirs along. He had to think about the seaworthiness of the contraption. After a while, he nodded approval. Next, Adam indicated with his fingers, the cross beams should not be paddle size but thicker. He should not have done that. Taos reacted just like Rona did at the festivities. Without saying a word, he left, leaving Adam wondering what he'd done wrong.

It was the bishop's turn now to walk up the hill to the master's place. In the first few days, they had only seen it from the beach or the hospital. The bishop had wondered why the master never showed up or invited him as the leader of the whites. That had changed now. Wayne had been there three times, for the bishop it was the second time and uninvited. Would he be received at all?

This time, a security person was on the trail again, but he was friendly, didn't say anything, and let he bishop pass. The master seemed to have waited for him. Perhaps somebody overheard the conversation during breakfast, down at their hut. They sat down and were served the obligatory coco milk by a nice young lady. Knowing of Wayne's adventure, the bishop wondered if she had been the one.

They talked about the weather, the fishing, and so on, as was the custom. The bishop figured, if somebody was down there who spoke English, the master would certainly have known of his visit today.

Lunch was served, this time on slivers of banana tree trunks. The bishop bowed his head and quietly said a prayer. The master did, too. That, of course, was an excellent opportunity for the bishop to return the conversation to the subject of religion. Staying on the island, and maybe forever, made converting the villagers to the right god his number one task.

He started right away with what bothered him most. "Your roots are a missionary station, not too far from here. But you, as the descendant, have no station, no workshop in which to do God's work with some of the tools, every workshop needs—you have no church as God's home."

He continued, "Every religion, not only Christianity, needs a place for the rituals like baptism, weddings, funerals, all the occasions of wonder, where we don't quite understand what's going on and have to trust a higher power that will make sure everything will be all right in the end. God will guide us; we are not alone. I don't see that here. Everybody is on his own, no church with trained officials to help the parishioners to find the right path through life and to God."

"You are right on all accounts. A community of Christians is like a quiver around arrows. When one arrow is about to break, not only the quiver but all the other arrows will keep it straight. It is, in fact, hard to be a Christian all by yourself, with no support group, no support in faith, and no support with mundane issues like being cared for when you are sick. We established the same institutions here as in the original missionary station, but no house of God. I never saw that as clearly as now, after you made me aware of this sin. I thank you."

The bishop was in cloud nine when he heard this. “I noticed that, and it is in fact what encouraged me to talk to you.” That was easier than in the bishop’s wildest dreams. “What can you do now?” he asked the master, “and how can I help?”

The master first took a sip from his coconut milk. He tended to weigh all options before he expressed his opinion.

The bishop was anxious to get a response but had to wait.

“Okay,” his host finally responded, “here is the whole story. I told you of our exodus from the original island, where my grandfather did his missionary work, but I didn’t go into much detail. I didn’t tell you which dark clouds are hanging over our family. Here it is:

“When my ancestors in the previous village were completely out of food, partly because of the refugees from the other village, they decided to become refugees themselves, just like the family that visited from up north. I told you that much. My grandfather organized the exodus. Early one morning, everybody who wanted to, assembled in the church. The people were asked to bring some tools and some plants and seeds for the start of a new colony on another island that wasn't as uninhabitable as theirs was after the cyclone. Inevitably, everybody brought the whole household. There weren't enough boats for all the people and their stuff. My grandfather had to call off the exodus."

The bishop couldn't wait to hear the rest of the story and how it related to the transformation of the Christian religion. So far, there was nothing new. When the master continued, he was quite obviously in pain with his confession.

"Next day, my grandfather called the church leaders, only those of his church, in his house. A secret meeting of just the elite and of only as many people as there were seats in the boats. At the same time, they restricted the items taken along to what a person could carry in one hand."

"Just the elite," the Bishop already sensed where this was going. That's exactly what gave the ultimate leadership of his church such a bad reputation from time to time.

The master was finally getting to the problem. "The party left at midnight in the cover of dark but made so much noise, the remaining villagers, those of slightly different belief, found out and were furious. A big fight between the two groups broke out. After a while, there were many injured people everywhere, maybe even some dead. It doesn't take much to kill a person half-dead from starvation."

The bishop knew, Christians fighting Christians had happened far too often in history.

The master continued, "At that point, my grandfather figured whoever was in a boat had to leave. There was no turning back. That's how they came here."

There was a long pause and several sips from the coconut bowl before the master finished the story with what happened on this island.

"Needless to say, my grandfather never stopped blaming himself for the bloodshed. He remained the leader of the flotilla, found the island here, but soon died from self-accusation. He was a broken man unable to govern with an iron fist, merging the two different views of Christianity as he should have in this brand-new colony. I personally think, he, himself, didn't believe in God anymore, after everything that had happened."

It was obvious the master was relieved to be able to tell somebody the sins of his forefathers. Hard to say if he thought of it as a confession, but he could have. He was speaking to a Catholic priest, after all.

End of story, the bishop figured, and he was right. The master's thoughts had finally turned from the long ago past to the present and the future.

"My father, the missionary's oldest son, was a teenager then, but immediately took over command. Nobody objected, because he was white and, therefore, superior. That's just the way it is and that explains why I would like to use the opportunity to get some brighter skin colour and European features back into the family."

"What a story," answered the bishop. "Although, I don't quite understand this skin colour ranking. Are we not all equal before God?"

"Yes, we are, but the islanders don't believe it."

The bishop decided to leave the issue of racism to Adam for now. Faith was more important, he figured. After all, it wasn't too long ago that coloured people all over the world were slaves. Nevertheless, at the time, Christianity flourished more than it does now.

He picked up the subject where they had left it. "What about religion, though, in this new place? Who changed the clear message of the Bible to something approaching camaraderie between the humans and their God?"

"When my father was about to build a church, there was a revolt among the people. They were upset with God. "What about all the slaughtered friends and family members," they asked. "Where was God then?" To make a long story short, no church was built and, by the time I became master, religion had changed into what it is now. It has been downgraded, but the people get along. Like my father and probably my grandfather, I feared, up to now, too much emphasis on religion would tear the community apart."

The bishop didn't want to stop there, with just an explanation and an apology. He did not accept status quo. "But it is no minor issue. It's between heaven and hell. Don't you think the two of us could try again? I think we are obliged to do so, to give it all we've got."

The master was undecided. He had not had enough time to think it over. "I don't even have a Bible," he said.

The bishop took that as a good sign. When somebody asks for tools, chances are, he's going to do the job. "I have one," the bishop was quick to not let this be a problem.

"I have never learned to read," confessed the master.

"I did," replied the bishop. "I'll be back tomorrow, with the Bible, if you don't mind."

The master was very tired. He just nodded. "Come back in the afternoon. I will have a nap before."

The bishop saw himself out in an excellent mood. He was about to convert and baptize about seventy people, and he would definitively go to heaven, not into hell, no matter what else he had done on earth.

CHAPTER 17

When the bishop came back, Henry and Mena, together with Reila, had just joined Adam. Henry laughed when he heard about Taos and his abrupt departure. “It’s pretty much like us giving the finger; only here, it’s not just the middle finger, all fingers count.” The whites were not as surprised now about similarities between both cultures as they were shortly after their arrival. They knew now that the ancestors of the present population had lived with white missionaries for some time and had picked up some customs and some words and expressions and had modified some of those.

Mena had brought the glossy picture book of Auckland. She wanted to know from the bishop and Adam if this was all real: the tall buildings, the cars and, most of all, the many people. It was unbelievable. "Yes, it is all real," she was told. Mena was glad she wouldn't have to go there. With the boat gone, she wouldn't have to decide and could live here with Henry, whom she called by his original name, Horam, again, and with Reila. There would be a second child, too, and she was very much looking forward to having a complete family.

Everybody knew there were other people in a world much bigger than just the island. After all, their ancestors had lived on a larger island and the descendants of the people staying there would very likely still live there. The missionaries at that distant time had come from somewhere and they had been white, like most of the people in those photographs and like the master and some members of his family. The firm belief that this outside world was dangerous was the main reason for not venturing out, exploring other lands.

Adam asked Henry to come with him to see Taos in order to clarify the finger situation. Taos accepted the apologies and sealed the cleansed relationship with a handshake, a gesture taken over from the white missionaries a long time ago.

Henry explained, in the local language, the design of a catamaran. Adam doubted whether Henry even knew what a proper cat was, but he hoped his version wasn't too far off. Taos nodded a few times and that looked promising. "Yes," he said, and Henry translated, "I have one canoe here I can use. The second one, I will have to make."

"Good, good. And how long will that take?"

"About four moons, if the weather co-operates."

Four months was out of the question. Adam didn't want to stay that long. "What about just an outrigger?"

How long would it take to make the outrigger? Taos thought it over. Finally, he came up with an estimate: one moon was his verdict.

"I now make them hollow, like the canoe itself. They are much more stable. I can hollow out trees. I do that for the canoes, why not for the outrigger? But I would have to find a proper way to seal the lid. Somebody, much earlier, designed the aqueduct to the hill, but it drips in places. I have to think about it." Adam was relieved. That sounded like he did understand.

In the meantime, quite a few villagers had gathered around them. Most of them were carrying a handmade bag or the all-purpose container, a coconut shell. When they figured the meeting with Taos was finished, they came forward, one after the other, and showed Adam the content. Pearls, pearls, they all brought their pearls to trade for something. Obviously, they figured, all the whites collected pearls. Wayne was the one interested in pearls. Adam told Henry he was not. Henry translated and then went farther up the creek, where he lived. Everybody else followed Adam down to the hospital area. It was quite a procession.

When they showed Wayne their treasures, he didn't know what to do, considering the drastically changed situation, after the boat had disappeared. If they had to stay here for years, maybe a lifetime, he would need everything he brought along. He would have nothing to trade. He said so to the bishop, the only person out of the three whites who didn't mind staying there and doing the missionary work.

The bishop had thought about the situation and came to a different conclusion. "If we stay here," he said, "we will not need most of our things, definitely no cloth. We must get integrated, behave, and dress like the locals. Otherwise, we will never be accepted and will always remain outsiders, not to be trusted."

Wayne had a closer look at the bishop and noticed he had changed into a skirt. "The master and I will have a little meeting with the chiefs. I can't be dressed better or more complete than the master."

Wayne was not yet convinced. If he never got back into civilization, all these pearls would be just toys again, as they were now. "What are our chances of going back?" he asked Adam, who was in an optimistic mood.

"Pretty good," Adam answered. "We will not have a catamaran but an outrigger."

"How many people can one canoe carry?"

"We have to test it, but three for sure, maybe four."

"We are five, six with Reila," Adam reminded him.

"I know, I know, but all we need is for somebody to get to the outside world. We know now where the island is. A helicopter will get whoever wants to come. Maybe even some locals."

"How do we pay for such a rescue mission?"

"That's where your pearls come in."

Wayne had one hundred and thirty-five of them, so far. Their value was completely unknown. The villagers were still standing around, ready to trade. The only person known to the whites was Rona. As if she had understood what was going on, she asked the men to line up and come forward with their pearls, one after the other. There were only men this time. It probably was too serious a business to let the women do it.

Wayne was not ready yet. He had learned quite a bit from the two buying sprees so far. He asked the sellers to show him how many pearls they had. Then he sorted those belongings he was ready to part with, according to the number of pearls in the hand of the villager, whose turn it was.

The trading session lasted for only half an hour. That was all the time Wayne had. It was getting dark, and he had to get ready for his nightly duty. He bought eighty-four pearls for four socks, a hat, and one shirt. He kept one to cover up his sunburn. Two sellers did not agree with the item he offered. They took their pearls back home again. That was the first time in living memory that a deal collapsed. It had the potential to stand the whole island economy on its head.

The same afternoon, the bishop paid a visit to the master as agreed. He found not only the master but all five chiefs, the leaders of the five villages. They were in the middle of the kava ceremony, and nothing was said for a while. Eventually the master welcomed him and asked him with gestures to sit down. Then he made a real presentation, in a style that rivalled any big business meeting. It was in the local language and the bishop didn't understand a word. Occasionally, the master pointed at the bishop, and every time the chiefs nodded politely. Then they were dismissed.

In their presence, no word was spoken in English. The chiefs didn't seem to know who spoke it and who didn't. Converting the lot to Christianity would be quite an undertaking. The bishop realized he was completely dependent on the master. If the master didn't co-operate, it would not happen. Henry would not help unless the master wanted him to. If Henry got involved against the order of the master, he would be out to sea again in a canoe and be looking for the coastguard to rescue him.

At the end of the meeting, after all the chiefs had left, the master explained to the bishop what he had told the chiefs. "Everybody here believes in Jesus Christ and is looking forward to join him in heaven. While here on earth, they just think that watching over all individuals and their tiny issues while at the same time organizing the stars in the universe is too much for one god, even if it's Jesus. That's where the guardian angels, the ancestors, come in, personal gods, that people can pray to. They are thought to be situated in the volcano. Nobody goes there and the myth continues.

Here is the plan now: If we could prove there are no gods at the volcano," the master continued, "we would be one step closer to the all-knowing God in the Bible. That would be the first step."

"And how do we do that?" the bishop wondered.

"We could all go there. That's what I asked the chiefs to prepare their clan members for. A trip to the volcano tomorrow. Our people are simple-minded. What they don't see is not there. We won't see any gods; that's for sure."

The bishop was not yet convinced. As long as they hadn't gotten rid of the ancestors, there would be no church and no regular service.

As if the master had read his thoughts, he continued, "The second step is trickier. We somehow must prove, Jesus has the capacity to watch over everybody on earth. He can do that all by himself. We still have to find a way how to get to this second step. We must think of something. Then we can build a church and worship together the one and only God, our Lord Jesus Christ."

When the bishop went down the trail after the meeting, it was pitch dark already. Wayne was just coming up. None of them was sure who the other person was. They didn't speak a word. They were just two shadows on the same trail but on a completely different mission.

CHAPTER 18

Wayne went into the same hut he had been the night before. He certainly was looking forward to the sex, holding the soft and warm body of a woman in his arms. There was, however, something else. The feeling was hard to describe. Maybe a professional poet would have had the words. Wayne the cab driver didn't. His feelings, however, were likely exactly the same. Expressed in simple language, it was a feeling like putting a lid on a jar. A feeling of belonging, of completing something, that, by itself, was incomplete.

The woman he was with the previous day was certainly not the first woman in his life. Wayne had been with quite a few. As a cab driver, he had to know all the watering holes in town. Taking the guests there was okay. Picking them up afterwards was sometimes more difficult, emotionally. Especially when it was a couple who had met in that place. Sex was in the air, almost palpable.

Sometimes he did go back to the outfit where he had picked up the passengers, to find a woman for himself. Most of the time, he was successful, sometimes not. These were all short-term relationships, a month, a week, more often just the night. Once he almost got married. That was a few years ago, and he had forgotten what went wrong.

When he entered the hut, the woman was there, just like the night before. Wayne had thought about this second encounter. He had fantasized all day and made plans. The second time, it should be easier, even more tender and loving than it was the first time, because both sides now knew their partner's reaction to the various parts of lovemaking.

It looked as if she had made plans for the night too, different ones. Her goal was quite obviously to get it over with. After about twenty minutes, she abruptly left. Wayne was torturing his brain to think of something that he had done wrong. He couldn't think of anything. In the end, he figured she just had a bad day or maybe two days in a row were too much. He would have to ask the master, if he should come again tonight or let a night lapse.

The other two whites were surprised when he got up with them early in the morning. They did, however, refrain from making comments about his lovemaking, and he didn't say anything, either. After breakfast, a villager appeared with one of Wayne's shirts. It was too wide. Wayne and the villager argued a while along the lines of "all sales are final." This was the villager's first purchase of anything. It was difficult without Henry's translation.

In a barter situation, something they were used to, if somebody didn't like the deal, the trade was simply reversed, period. They could have done that, too, but Wayne wanted to keep the pearls. Finally, Adam ended the standoff. He suggested to Wayne to give back the twelve pearls the shirt originally cost and, in turn, get his shirt back. Then he, Adam, would sell one of his smaller shirts to the villager for sixteen pearls, a profit for the whites of four pearls. The poor man did not have more pearls and was, therefore, four pearls in debt to Adam. Wayne started an account, the first on the island. He sold his wider shirt the same day for the newly established price of sixteen pearls a shirt.

Adam needed the pearls to give to Taos. Taos had indicated the day before that he really liked pearls as payment and would not want any cloth or other item, no shirt. He didn't want to wear one, since he was sweating so much with his hard work.

Soon Adam realized, so far, he was the only one helping with the construction of the outrigger. Wayne wanted to be in it for sure and, therefore, had to contribute all or part of his pearls. But what about the others? Adam needed at least a second person to make it through the current; four would be better. The bishop and Henry, plus family, were a maybe. How could they pay for a maybe? And how would Henry pay when he had no pearls?

As the day went on, Adam and Wayne were busier and busier with trades. Pretty much all villagers, this time the women, too, came to trade. Many more pearls were around than Wayne had expected. They came from those huts Wayne hadn't been to yet but also from places where he had been. He had been tricked. With so many more pearls around, prices for all the whites' stuff went up. In fact, Wayne bought some of the articles, sold yesterday, back again. Most of the time, his customers were sorry to do so, but reversing a trade within a reasonable time was still the law.

At the end of the day, Wayne and Adam had together 241 pearls. That was a huge amount, considering they, themselves, had only one purchase to make: the canoe. Whatever was left had to pay for the chopper, if that became a fixed component of their escape plan.

There were too many unknowns for Adam's taste. They had only the number of pearls as a fixed amount. They had no idea how much they were worth and how much the helicopter would be. They also didn't know how much they would have to pay to Taos. That, however, could be found out. They both went up to Taos's hut and asked him. The language barrier appeared again and in a big way, but they managed. Taos's math didn't go far enough to come up with a number, but he had a clear idea about the worth of his work. He went inside the hut and came out again with half a coconut shell. That should be filled with pearls, and then they were even. It was quite clear that thing would swallow all their pearls.

In all this frantic trading activity, Wayne had forgotten to ask the master about tonight. It was too late now; he had to go up there and see what the situation was. He could not find the master in the dark, but he did find the hut he had been in twice. Sure enough, the woman was there. No need to ask the master. The girl felt a bit different today. She had cut her hair short and was much more active than she had been the day before. For a little while, Wayne ignored the changes but in the end, he had to admit, this was a different woman.

It suddenly dawned on him that he had slept with three different women. They were probably the three the master had picked, when he had hoped all three whites would get involved in the gene pool update. Wayne realized, theoretically, he could become the father not only of one child but three. If he and his comrades got away from the island, it would be okay. If not, he would have three wives and might as well convert to Islam, and be lost to the bishop's Christianity.

Again, Wayne was back in the white men's quarters in the evening, as in the night before and up the next morning, just in time to join the villagers, ready to walk up to the volcano.

CHAPTER 19

Not everybody went up the trail along the creek to find the gods. Kids were deposited in the daycare by their mothers. As always, Rona volunteered to supervise them. When asked if she didn't want to find her god, she replied, "I'm sure taking care of the kids will be appreciated by God, wherever he is."

There were the sick and old people, those who got their meals down at the hospital. They didn't go. More significant was the medicine man who did not come, either. No reason given, but the whites had noticed some time ago that no love was lost between the medicine man and the master. They figured, with so much power to the master, the medicine man could never truly fulfill his function as spiritual leader. They didn't know the island's population well enough to see who else was missing. Henry told them, that quite a few stayed home. In a way, the trip was also a power struggle between the master and the medicine man.

The whole procession moved slowly up the creek trail. Soon, the last village, the one where Mena lived, lay behind them. She joined, too. The trail became steeper and steeper as they got closer to the volcano. Some people didn't have the strength to continue and had to quit and stay back. Henry, who knew all the villagers, noticed some villagers quit, although they certainly had the strength. They faked weakness to get out of this dangerous adventure. To confront your god while you are still on earth and alive takes some courage.

The master had to quit and gave the command over to his oldest son, his most likely successor. At his age, he didn't have the energy for about a ninety-minute walk up, and up, and then down again. At this point, like a mirage, the medicine man joined the expedition. He was either coming up a different trail or he was running behind. Either way, he had been waiting for this change in leadership. The master's son was no match for him.

Although the whites were living close to the medicine man's hut and his hospital, they had never spoken to him more than good morning or good night. They had the impression that man, if he could, he would have sent them out in an instant on the ocean in a single canoe to their certain death. And seen from his point of view, he was right. So far, the intruders, as he called them, had strengthened the master's position tremendously. They were even about to help create the next generation of masters. He knew where Wayne spent his nights and how. Today's adventure was the height of their interference in island matters. Never would the master have had the insolence to lead a procession into the sacred land of the gods without encouragement by the one white they called the bishop.

Soon the trail was "littered" with lame hikers; only about twenty of the original forty soldiered on. Those still marching started to question the purpose of the walk. There was no upside, just a risk. Most of them were happy with their personal gods. If they met them up there, the gods would definitely be upset, and who knew what kind of punishment they had in store.

If they didn't find gods there, they were safe for now but might have insulted the Christian god just by looking for others. Why, then, would they continue? They would have to build a church and start praying to Jesus Christ in addition to their own god. They continued walking only because the chiefs had told them to.

The moment the master turned around, the bishop became very worried about the mission. God was a power to feel inside, not something to be seen in a volcano, of all places. If he only spoke the language and could talk to the people. He felt he had to give it a try. When the group rested again, as they did more often now, he found Henry and asked him to translate. "Dear congregation," he started, "we are assembled here in the name of the Lord. We are about to convince ourselves that there are no other gods than Jesus Christ."

Henry did his best in translating, but half of the words like "congregation" and "assembled" he did not know in the island's language.

The medicine man used the pause to start praying to his god with his thundering voice. Other people fell to their knees and prayed. The master's son spoke, ordering to continue with the walk, but he could not make himself heard in the overall noise. Everybody was speaking now, praying or otherwise. Somebody was praying to Jesus, asking him not to let his personal god punish him.

At that point, the volcano that everybody thought was extinct started to rumble and the earth underneath their feet shook. The fact the mountain did it at this crucial moment was seen as a sign by everybody. But what for? Was it to encourage the people with a personal god down in the volcano, not to come any closer? Or was the one Christian god threatening the unbelievers with the hell fire? Or was it just the unrest of the magma inside the volcano, taking a breather?

Time to go back, either to pacify the gods or simply not to get caught in a major eruption of the volcano. They went home in three groups, more or less, according to their beliefs in Jesus as the one, led by the bishop, or the familiar personal god, led by the medicine man. The third group, walking way behind, consisted of all those whose feet were blistered in their flimsy sandals. The master, when he was told how everything went wrong, decided to groom the second son as his successor instead of the oldest.

CHAPTER 20

The following day, Rona and Adam happened to be the last ones at the breakfast table. Everybody else had something more important to do. Not Adam. He could have spent all day in Rona's company, no matter what she was doing, and she was always doing something. No break in work for her; yet, she was always the happiest girl around. With the two of them being alone, Rona could practice her English. It was quite good, considering she could only use it in contact with the master's family. "Don't tell anybody," she had told Adam some time ago.

Turning to Adam, she asked, "How was it yesterday, your trip up the trail?"

"There was a palpable tension and a division of the whole village into different groups. I don't think that's good for such a small population. The people are dependent on each other and should stand together. The trail, however, is beautiful; everything is in bloom and, if not, at least the leaves are green in an unbelievable number of shades."

"I haven't been up there for years."

"Why don't you go, then? Is it because you can't set aside a few hours with all the work here?"

"No, no, I could leave here for a few hours. Mena could take over for a while, no problem."

"What's holding you back, then?"

"I don't want to go alone."

Well, that could be helped. On the island, offering a walk into the bush to a man was like asking one in the city to come up for a cup of coffee, after a night out in town.

"Let's go together, then."

Rona finished what she was doing, then packed a lunch, and they went. When they came to Mena's place, Rona asked her to take care of things down at the main village.

Adam appreciated Rona's clever idea to be alone with him. In order just to talk about something, he asked her if she didn't want to go alone because she was afraid of the gods up there.

"Oh, no," she answered, "I'm not afraid of gods up there." She pointed to the volcano. "Neither am I of a god up there." She pointed to the sky.

"Where is your god, then?"

"Inside of me."

"How would that work? Do you pray to yourself?"

"I don't. I don't pray."

They were sneaking by the water manager, who was sleeping next to his basin. Water was plenty. It had rained early in the morning, which was quite unusual.

While Adam was still trying to understand how any belief would work without praying, Rona continued, "I did pray as a child, until I found out praying doesn't make any difference. You might feel better, but whatever you prayed for happens or doesn't anyway. With every other action, people watch the outcome. If one way to reach their objective doesn't work, they try something else. With praying, it's different. If God doesn't listen to their prayers, they still continue. What's even more astounding, the less God fulfills their wishes, lets them suffer, even, the more they need him and the more they pray."

The two youngsters had reached in half the time the spot where the procession the day before had turned around. They were hiking the steeper section of the trail now. What had started as small talk had turned into something very serious.

"Take my sister Mena, and me, for instance," Rona picked up the subject again, "and the ups and downs we went through. Our father died in a logging accident when we were young girls. One strike against both of us. Then our mother died from a mysterious illness; we still don't know what it was. Maybe fish poisoning. Strike two. Mena is a year and a half older than I am. She was allowed to live by herself in our family hut. Good for her. I was made, what you call, a foster child, same as you have been. Bad for me, because the family they put me in was not nice.

The husband molested me and the mother made me work all day."

Before Adam could feel sorry for her, the situation was improving.

"Eventually, I was adopted by the master. They needed somebody to care for the sick and old people. That was good for me. I had learned to work hard at the foster family and I like to help the weak members of the community. Living with the master's family is where I learned to speak English. Yes, there was a school on the hill, but there are no more young kids in the master's family and that's why there is none today."

Rona had asked the master, begged him to allow her to set up a school for the village kids. He had rejected it. No reason given.

She had stopped talking, still upset about the lack of a formal education for all kids but now continued. "Soon Mena picked Henry as husband. That was good for her, but only for a short time. Then Henry was banned and she was all alone with the tiny baby. Really bad for her. Now Henry is back. Good for her, but how will their life continue and where, with the boat gone? Now you tell me, where is God in all of that?"

At this point, Adam was in his element. This kind of discussion he was used to from the youth group. "Life is not fair. Never was. That's why there are religions in order to compensate after death all the misery on earth. All religions have a reward system of one kind or another, not just Christians. It's what keeps people behaving according to what, in Christianity, are the Ten Commandments. You follow them and you get rewarded in heaven. If not, you get punished."

While he was talking, Adam had noticed their discussion had left the right track, as the bishop would say. Sins are forgiven, when you believe. They are not the problem. Adam had not only read the novels in the bishop's library, but he had also studied the Bible. There, in John 14:6 it says: "no man cometh onto the father, but by me." Adam had often wondered what was more important: to be good or to be faithful; to behave or to believe. Or did it have to be both. According to John, without believing Rona had no chance in hell, so to speak, to ever get rewarded in heaven.

He wondered how she saw that and asked, "But how do you expect to ever get rewarded for all the good you do? You don't believe in God. To me that means, you don't believe in heaven. When and where will you get your rewards?"

"This is one of the reasons why it's convenient to have God inside. When I help others, I get rewarded right away by feeling good inside. No waiting period."

Adam wasn't convinced. "That seems to me a kind of consolation prize compared to heavenly rewards." Despite all the time he had spent in the bishop's household, he did not know exactly what the reward system was. Maybe it was just not being punished in hell. "What, if you do go to hell?" he asked.

"There will be lots of good people in heaven to bail me out because I helped them on earth," she said with a twinkle in her eyes.

Adam sensed she wasn't quite sure about her perspective of good and bad and how or whether it is rewarded and where. He knew most people aren't, and that included himself.

Adam wanted to continue with their conversation. "How about me?" he asked. "Now I am in your life and you are loved so much. Is that good or bad?"

"It's wonderful," she replied, grabbing him by the arm, and dragging him to a place away from the trail. The spot might have been close to where Henry and Mena spent three days. They didn't have three days, only about three hours but enjoyed every minute of it. They had been in love for some time, but this was the first time they touched each other. The lunch, they took along, was never touched.

CHAPTER 21

When not preoccupied with matters of love, Adam spent a lot of time with Taos, helping him to hollow out that tree for the newly invented hollow outrigger. Maybe it didn't have to be hollow. The fishermen's weren't. He wished he had brought his chainsaw. With it, the rough parts could have been done in only one or two hours. He also wondered how they would get the finished canoe down to the water. There was no way to find out because of the solid language barrier. No Henry in sight to translate.

Wayne started his pearl business again. He bought pearls in exchange for personal belongings. But he also returned pearls in this exchange program whenever he felt he could make a profit. The fact they had to give so many pearls to Taos dampened his enthusiasm a bit, but he hoped he could convince Taos to receive something else for his canoe building efforts.

The bishop and the master were wandering the grounds up on the hill looking for a level spot where they could build a church. As a first step, they built a fence. They used freshly cut trees as fence posts and finished it with bamboo mats hung between these posts. That didn't take long. All the master's family members helped. Some villagers helped, too, but not many, and that worried the bishop. He had counted on more support, not so much for building the church but for attendance to the service later.

Service itself was problematic. The bishop would read from the Bible, but would there be anybody to translate? The master didn't want to give away that he was bilingual. Would he get Henry to translate? Parts would simply be presented in English only, drawing their importance and sense of urgency from the bishop's voice alone as it was, when everything in church was presented in Latin.

While the bishop was busy on the hill and Adam and Henry up the trail with Taos, it came as a big surprise to Wayne when the medicine man started to walk the ground close to the hospital. He also marked a square with posts. More and more villagers joined him. Wayne didn't trust his eyes when he saw they were building an enclosure, exactly like the one he could see going up on the hill.

Wayne gestured to the medicine man, pointing to the structure on the hill. The medicine man just grinned and continued. Luckily, Henry came along the path. He asked the medicine man what the purpose was and got a short answer. "Oh, we accept the bishop's advice to pray all together." Henry and Wayne wondered why the villagers would have to use two fenced areas, one up the hill and one down here. But they were glad there would be unity again.

The division was hurting Wayne's pearl business. So many of his potential customers were now busy setting up walls. Henry sensed something else and asked, "So, you are accepting that there is only one god you can all pray to?"

"Why would we do that?" was the medicine man's reply. "Share one god when we can each have our own, serving our needs?" Nothing had changed. Henry translated for Wayne.

Wayne was not religious, but he realized there was still a fundamental difference between the one view of God and the other. He remembered from attending Bible school, as a kid, it wasn't about God serving the people, it was they who served God. That's why the worship on Sundays was also called "service." What for a moment looked like unification had now turned into the power struggle again between the master with the bishop on one side and the medicine man and most of the villagers on the other.

Wayne was not sure if the medicine man's construction could be seen from the hill above. He figured the bishop should know and decided to close his trading post temporarily and walk up the hill to tell him. On the way, he met Rona. Their close relationship had ended long ago when Wayne accepted to sleep with the master's girls. They were still friendly with each other when

Rona served meals, and so on. Now they were talking about the two buildings and different views of religion until it hit Wayne like a rock. They spoke in English. Rona also spoke English, something Adam knew already but couldn't tell the others. That immediately solved a puzzle that had frustrated him and the bishop all along. She was the master's spy in the village. That's how he knew everything they did and talked about.

The master and the bishop already knew what was going on down there. They hadn't seen it at first but when the hammering of posts into the ground started, they did hear it and looked. The two leaders had decided to go on with their project, regardless.

Helping with the construction were a few young women, members of the master's family. Some good-looking ones, too. Wayne wondered with whom he had slept and in what order. He had a rough idea who they were. One, he liked more than the others. Was she the one from the first night? He hoped so.

There was no way to find out when Sunday was. Nobody had a calendar. The whites, with the help of Henry, tried to count forward from their day of arrival, which was a Tuesday, but none of them was sure how many nights had passed. They asked around, if somebody remembered. The villagers didn't understand why they wanted to know. Was not one day like the other and that was good so? They knew the phases of the moon and counted longer periods like a year by its waning and waxing, and that was good enough.

Not to lose any time, the bishop declared the following day to be Sunday and Sunday worship. He invited everybody to attend. But at what time? People that don't care about days and time in general had no use for the measurement of hours. They could have had a sun dial but didn't. Hundreds of years ago, in Europe, people didn't know the time of day, either. That's where the church bells came in. There were no bells here but drums and the master's trombone. It would finally serve for church services, again, as it had done such a long time ago. Word was spread.

Up on the hill, the master's family and about two dozen other villagers convened. Down by the hospital the fenced area at the hospital could not hold all the worshippers. Some were inside, some outside. Somebody suggested to do away with the fence altogether. After all, their praying wasn't confidential. They had openly done it for generations.

They tore the fence down. The medicine man felt a bit foolish for adopting something the bishop had recommended. He recovered when he was the first one to bend his head to pray and everybody else followed immediately. After about fifteen minutes, he rose and left, and so did everybody else. On the hill, the bishop's voice could be heard for about an hour. Henry did not go to either of the services.

CHAPTER 22

The next few days were uneventful. Adam continued his work with Taos. The outrigger part of the boat was taking shape. The bishop learned a few sentences in the local language from Henry. He figured a few sentences would be appreciated as goodwill. There is a problem, though, with that method of learning, by putting a string of sounds together, without knowing the basics.

Somebody may figure you actually speak the language and ask you a simple question, which you don't understand. You start guessing and, often, with your inappropriate answer, you look like a fool. That's the end, then, of the good impression you wanted to make.

Wayne went up the hill to ask the master if he should continue sleeping with the three girls. He knew that babies were not always made with one shot. The master would certainly know that, too. Wayne didn't want to withdraw his services altogether. What he really wanted was to sleep with the first woman as often as possible and to skip the others. She was so cute, so soft, so warm. Wayne could fall in love with her if he wasn't already. If she was the pretty girl he had seen as part of the construction crew, he might even take her with him and get married. That was, if they ever got away from that place. If not, would he marry her here?

The master's decision was that he should come every second day, starting today. There would always be the same woman waiting for him, but he did not say which one it was. Would it be number one, two, or three? That was okay with Wayne. He would know for sure after this night. If it was number two or three, he might reconsider.

The master had spread the word: there would be services every Sunday now, and he would remind the parishioners on Saturday that the following day was such a Sunday. The master and the bishop also let it be known there would be pearls distributed to everybody attending. These were pearls the bishop had bought from Wayne for the promise of buying him a pair of jeans, if they ever got home. If they didn't, none of them needed pearls.

The bishop had not yet contributed any personal belongings while Wayne and Adam were pretty bare, as far as clothing was concerned. To convert all the villagers would take quite some time, the bishop figured. In all that time, he would need proper cloth to be respectable. Meeting the chiefs in a skirt at that recent meeting was embarrassing since the master wore pants on that occasion.

Sunday came and a huge crowd assembled up on the hill while only a small group of villagers gathered at the medicine man's place. Some people went to the latter, bowed, prayed for a minute, and then ran up the trail to the hill to get the promised pearls.

Among the small group of people joining the medicine man was Adam. He was infuriated. The bishop was buying votes for pearls and that could not be tolerated. He did not know how many pearls were promised to the hill people, but he knew the number of pearls given to the bishop. That divided by the estimated one-god crowd up the hill resulted in about two pearls per person.

Adam went to the whites' hut and came back with Wayne's treasure: all his pearls. Everybody believing in a personal god, those joining the medicine man, received eight pearls. As it turned out, because of the huge crowd on the hill, everybody there received only one pearl. The master's family members got none. There weren't enough. A lot of parishioners were not happy with their gift. It had been said "pearls," plural, would be given, not just one.

CHAPTER 23

The following day, the master came down into the village looking for the bishop. He wasn't happy. Something had gone wrong. Chief Pug, Mena's clan leader and for now Henry's, had filed suit against the bishop for bribery. Pug was a troublemaker and everybody knew it. Two years ago, he was mostly responsible for Henry's ban. Now he claimed the promise of pearls had lured people to decide for a way of religion, which they otherwise wouldn't have supported. Pug did that on behalf of the medicine man, who wanted to stay in the background for now. He knew, if the master continued to promote this Bible-based religion, they would clash some day and in a big way. For now, he attacked a softer target, the bishop.

There was not much the master could do about it. He had to call a court session for later in the afternoon. The trombone and drums would indicate at what time. All the chiefs had to come, likewise the bishop, the accused. Adam was sorry for having gotten involved in this pearl giveaway, but bribes he could not tolerate. Fairness was very high up on his list of virtues. As for the payment in pearls to Taos, there never were enough pearls to fill the cup, anyway.

When they heard the trombone, pretty much everybody came. Those court proceedings were the only big entertainment on the island. Mena, in her time of loneliness, had not missed any. Today, she was there, too, with Henry again, and that reminded both of Henry's trial and his last hours on the island. This time, the accused was the bishop. Henry had to sit next to him as his translator. Without Henry, the bishop would be out to sea in a canoe on his way to a certain death. Eventually, water would do him in, either too much, the ocean, or the lack of it, drinking water. The accused had never in his life sat in a canoe.

There were fixed rules for court proceedings. The master said a few words, not unlike "Court is in session." Then chief Pug stated his accusation of bribery towards the bishop because of the pearls he had promised and also given away. The master had made that same promise, but he was immune.

Next, Pug called witnesses. Everybody who had been in the enclosure up on the hill testified that the promise of pearls had motivated them to join the master and the bishop, and not the medicine man. They had been bribed to attend. It did not look good for the manipulating bishop.

At the end of that witness section, within the standardized court proceedings, Henry's translation lasted much longer than before. "Look," he said to the bishop, "you don't have a defender; therefore, you are entitled to call your own witnesses. You must remind the court that the medicine man gave out eight pearls. Against such competition, you would not have been able to lure a single person to the one pearl event up hill."

The bishop was shaking, scared for his life. Any sentence was a death sentence. He knew that. He was too scared to understand what Henry was saying. When the bishop didn't say anything, Henry said to him, "Say the Ten Commandments." The bishop did that with a cracking voice. Henry translated it to mean, "The accused wants to call his witnesses." Henry then called several witnesses, who had attended the service down in the village. They all testified the offer of one pearl could not have been a bribe, when everybody at the medicine man's place received eight.

These witnesses had before received six pearls from the master for their testimony when all they had to do was to say the truth. Adam was relieved. The way it looked, his spontaneous eight-pearl gift had saved the bishop's life. But the session was not over yet.

Quite a few family members of the master were in attendance. Some of them wondered about Henry's translation of the commandments but, luckily, they were all on the bishop's side and kept their mouths shut.

The court was deadlocked. For both events, bribes had been given to influence the decision of where to go. That gave the master an opportunity to declare the session closed with the bishop found not guilty, as always, when in doubt. The question of timing simply didn't come up. The fact that those people up on the hill had expected to be given pearls, a bribe, while those in the village could not have known they would get any when they made their decision of where to go. The master told the bishop later, he did have a plan and would never have found the bishop guilty. He did not, however, elaborate what plan that was.

CHAPTER 24

The master and the bishop had lots to talk about. So far, the success of their mission had been less than expected. The bishop was always coming or going in the master's quarters to talk strategy. Running up the trail was the only way to find out if the master had time to listen to his endless ideas. Sometimes, the master wished he had not agreed to the bishop's mission. Nevertheless, living far apart was inconvenient for both men. The master invited, therefore, the bishop to move into his quarters. He would always inform the bishop about when he had time for their project.

To offer something to the master's family in return, the bishop offered Bible studies for the women and for the kids, boys and girls separately, and also separately for different age groups. The boys between fourteen and seventeen were his favorite group. He was disappointed when he learned, presently, there were no school age kids on the hill. The youngest members of the master's family were the young women, Wayne's playmates. The bishop's interest waned quickly.

Wayne had found out, during his next visit, his love was, in fact, "number one," Goranda, by name. He was out of his mind with joy. "Were the other two your sisters?" he asked her.

"I'm not supposed to tell, but they weren't. They didn't want to have a mixed-race baby and an absentee father."

"But I was together with two other women. Who were they?"

"I shouldn't have told you. All the other young women wanted to know how it is with a white man."

"How did they pick the ones?"

"They drew straws."

"Does the master know?"

"For heaven's sake, don't ever tell him."

"It will come out anyway, when babies show."

"None of them is pregnant. Neither am I." She turned to Wayne with a sly smile. "When it comes to our bellies, we women are fully in control."

The master wanted to strengthen the band of at least one white with his family and, therefore, allowed the lovebirds to move permanently into the hut, where they had spent the nights. That meant Wayne could finally have an open relationship with the soft, mild mannered, and now soft-spoken, girl whom he had seen at the church construction.

Adam was alone now in the hospital building. He didn't mind and even started to redecorate the interior. Rona visited whenever she had time. Adam spent most of his time with Taos anyway, working on the boat. He even learned some rudimentary local language. Wayne joined them at the construction site less and less frequently. He had become very fast a member of the master's family with chores to do.

The co-operation with the family members was interesting. Oftentimes, there was a clash of practical experience on the side of the family versus theoretical knowledge from the outside world contributed by Wayne. For instance, the villagers did not use wheels. They knew there used to be wheels on the original island, but nobody here had ever used one. The terrain was too uneven to tow a cart over all the rocks that were sticking out everywhere. Wayne figured that might be true, but what about a wheelbarrow with just one wheel? He hacked a slice from a tree trunk and drilled a hole for the axle with a strong knife. It did work, but not for long. A wheel with spokes would have been better.

The two seniors, the master and the bishop, tried to think of a miracle, which would convince the people of the real power of God. They, themselves, did not doubt in God's abilities. He could work miracles. But not on command and not always. Sometimes his timing was off. They needed a miracle now. Suddenly the master had an idea. "We get the boat back; that's it. We furiously pray in the presence of pretty much everybody and ask God to give your boat back."

The bishop was sitting there with an open mouth. "What?" he said eventually. "The boat is still here?"

"Oh yeah," the master continued, "it never was out of reach. My boys put it into a safe place. Don't you worry about it."

"But all our future was dependent on having a boat or not. It was our only way back to civilization. Don't you think you should have told us, or at least me?" The bishop was faced with a prime example of how the master controlled everything.

He did explain, though. "Well, at that point, we weren't friends and confidants yet. And besides, I would have told you when the time was right and you were ready to go. I don't see that to be the case now. Wayne is happy with Goranda, you are on an incomplete mission to save souls, and Henry belongs here anyway, together with wife and child. That leaves just Adam. He can not run a boat by himself. With the boat, we have a tool now to get them all to our side and finish off with a big baptism celebration. Then you take your boat home with everybody who wants to come."

The bishop was glad but also disappointed, or was he disappointed more than glad? He couldn't quite decide what his priorities were. The order of things was, however, like the master had said,: first the conversion based on a miracle, then the trip back,—with whom, only time would tell.

The two men continued plotting the big event. They would have to organize a gathering where everybody, no matter what belief, would want to participate. They wanted to have as many witnesses as possible, hoping for all adults. Then they would pray for the return of the boat. Next morning, it would be back at its old mooring as if it had never had been away. That final step was the biggest challenge in the bishop's mind. He said so, and the master just waved his hand, discarding the bishop's concern. "My boys will bring it back exactly as they have put it away."

The big event that they came up with was a reunion of sorts, where the medicine man and the bishop would pray to both versions of God. Jesus would be seen as the boss who controlled everything, while the gods up on the volcano were his assistants and did their best for each individual believer, to whom they were assigned. It was okay, then, to pray to Jesus first, but when he didn't respond, because he was busy otherwise, to turn to his assistants, the ancestors, for help. The bishop had no problem with this version because all his life he had prayed to Mary, in her function as assistant to her son.

The master spread the word and since everything on this small island was either done right away or not at all, it was called for the following day. Pearls would also be handed out. Wayne agreed to give up all his remaining pearls. There weren't enough for Taos anyway. Adam had to think of something else as pay. He had not yet been told about the miraculous re-appearance of the boat. The bishop had not told Wayne, either, because lovebirds tend to give away secrets faster than you can snap your fingers. He didn't trust Henry either because, after several weeks back, where he grew up, he was torn between the brown and the white members of society. He might tell Mena.

The big event came. Pretty much all adults were there. The medicine man, too, and everybody was relieved that a common ground had been found. First, the bishop prayed to the almighty, then to his individual god; that's at least how Henry translated it, but he didn't, really. He prayed to Mary. Obviously pacified, the medicine man prayed to both, as it was agreed as a compromise. Finally, the master prayed, too. "Our

Father, who art in heaven, hallowed be thy name. Your kingdom come...and please help us recover the big boat that our friends have come with. Please put it back into the same spot, where it was, before you took it for safekeeping. And thank you, Jesus, amen."

Some people prayed hesitantly with him, but most didn't know the words anymore, if they ever did.

CHAPTER 25

The fishermen were always the first to get up at dawn. They did so the following morning as well. But none of them went out fishing. They were standing around the white people's boat that had miraculously re-appeared. It was tied to the same two trees as before. It was the same boat for sure. There had been some dents and scratches in the aluminum, which made it easy for the fishermen to identify it as the original, the one that had disappeared. The dents and scratches made them assume the boat wasn't as sturdy as their wooden canoes, but it was definitely the same boat.

There was one minor difference. The boat had blood stains in three places. Where did they come from? Did Jesus hurt himself on some sharp edges of the boat or the rocks? The villagers had lots of experience with rocks but did not know aluminium boats.

Word spread and soon everybody was down on the beach, as if they had never seen such a boat. It wasn't the boat, though, that they admired. It was the miracle they were looking at. The day before, the master had asked God, the Jesus god, to bring the boat back and he did. That was power. To have such a friend was unbeatable.

As the last ones, the master and his family came down to see the wonder. Only the oldest son was missing. Also missing was the medicine man. He was treating a deep cut in the left leg of the master's oldest son. Finally, the medicine man joined all the others. "A miracle, look, a miracle," he was told. "Just yesterday the master prayed to Jesus Christ to bring back the boat and he did."

As a professional healer, the medicine man immediately saw the blood stains on the boat. He knew where they came from and had a pretty good idea whose blood it was. He had already treated the wound, back in his hospital. And it wasn't Jesus Christ, whose leg he stopped from oozing blood, it was the master's oldest son's. No need to "treat" anything other than to treat this betrayal with disgust. He turned to the master and with his loudest voice screamed, "You liar, you charlatan; there is no miracle here. Your oldest son, who most likely also hid the boat, brought it back. He hurt himself on a sharp rock. That's all."

The mob would have lynched anybody who had betrayed the whole community on the spot or at least send him out in a leaky canoe and banned him from coming back. To overcome their respect for the master took a little longer. They even listened to him when he asked for silence. Then he explained, "Who says there is betrayal here? You do betray somebody by hiding the truth, basically by lying. This is not what happened here. I never told you Jesus brought back the boat. He didn't; my sons did. And do you know why? They followed the wise man's saying: "help themselves, so help you God." When they realized this morning that God had other priorities, they prayed again and asked God to at least get the boat close to the island and to please let them know where to look for it."

"He did, and they found it and got it. From yesterday's prayer, they knew I wanted it. They did it out of love for me."

He demonstratively hugged the son who was present. "Thank you, thank you so much. Now I can help our guests get home, and helping others is seen by God as service to him." The master knew declaring God as overworked and unable to bring the boat back all the way would strengthen the case for individual gods, but he had to come up with something.

Then he and his family retreated slowly up the hill. They took the wounded son with them, half carrying him, half dragging him. The master asked his oldest son why he didn't come to him with his wound but to the medicine man. "We always go to him," was the weak answer, "and it did bleed a lot." This was the second time this son failed the family. The master finally decided to make the second son his successor. Would there be a succession after this lack of leadership?

This was the medicine man's hour. He told the still-listening crowd, "A liar, he is, nonetheless. He said the boat was carried away by the storm, when in fact, he knew all along that it was hidden some place. Don't believe a word of what he is saying."

Followed by at least half the population, he marched up the village trail and pointed out the huts of those families who believed in and prayed to the only god, Jesus Christ, and not to the gods in the volcano. On some of the huts, they pulled out a pole or tore off part of the thatched roof. Most huts were not very well built, since no proper building material was available like on the previous island. Nothing was nailed or screwed on; every connection was tied together. The crowd would have done more damage to the flimsy huts, but the medicine man walked at a steady pace and didn't give them enough time to do much damage.

When they came to Taos's house, Adam asked the medicine man to spare it. It was true, Taos had not come to any of the medicine man's events. He was an unbeliever, not interested in any god. However, Adam, the one asking on Taos behalf, had always fought against the ruling family and their presumptions. During all his time on the island, he had supported the women and the weak. The medicine man, who had closely watched his white neighbours living next to him at the hospital and who had seen some of Adam's social actions, especially for women, declared Taos's house safe.

Next and last up the creek was Henry's and Mena's place. The mob stopped short of going there. Henry was believed to be a formidable fighter, although that had never been proven. He was, however, the only banned person to come back, which would have required unbelievable strength. In any case, he would have had the support from three whites. You never knew what weapons these guys had. The revolutionists turned around.

Mena had no interest at all in the power struggle. The master had banned Henry, but the medicine man would have, too. He probably wouldn't have allowed Henry to return. The master did. Henry had been neutral so far. He had seen on TV so much human suffering from wars, much more actually than from natural disasters like earthquakes, tsunamis and outbreaks of volcanoes. To have a fight because of differences about a religion was beyond him. In their case, it was not even a completely different path to God. It was the same god and the same basic religion they were fighting about.

Henry had discussed this issue with Adam, the reader, who knew almost everything from books. Henry had asked Adam, "Why does one group of people with a slightly different view of God fight another and not, instead, pity everybody who is on the wrong path? After all, these poor, misguided creatures might not make it into heaven. They should be pampered here on earth, to make up for their suffering in hell, not be fought against or even be killed."

Adam in his wisdom explained, "It is not about religion; it's about power. And besides, as a French philosopher whose name has slipped my mind once said: 'there is no easier way to justify a cruelty, than doing it in the name of God.'"

Suspecting more trouble to come, many of the "one god Christians" decided to break house and to move up the hill to the master. Some set up their huts there; others found refuge in the existing buildings. Wayne's love nest now housed a family of six. He and Goranda moved in with one of the master's other girls. Wayne wondered whether she was number two or three or not involved at all.

Later in the evening, a group of people, about a dozen, came up the hill to do the same damage, or worse, to the buildings there. The master told the family and refugees to stay inside. He ordered the sons to get ready for battle, but only if he was down or gave them a signal. Then he went outside to confront the would-be attackers. There he stood: praying to God, the only one. The old magic still worked. The leader of the crowd turned around and left, taking everybody with him, not without promising to come back.

The master was a brave man, considering his age, but he was even more clever than brave. The leader of the group coming up was, like Rona, a spy for him. A crowd like this is always looking for a leader. It is so easy to stir them in any direction. The master's family and guests saw it as great power and became a bit more hopeful again for their future.

The medicine man was the master's equal in every way. He figured he didn't have to get into a fight with the small but still strong group of people up at the master's. All he had to do was to destroy the aqueduct carrying water to the people there. Without drinking water, they would soon give up and agree to his terms. He would be the new master and ban from the island anybody he found not following his new rules. The villagers were probably not yet quite ready for such a drastic measure. There was a drawback to this method, too. The aqueduct would have to be rebuilt once he was living up there. Who would do that? He could wait, though; time was on his side, especially now that the whites would be leaving again.

CHAPTER 26

Down at the distribution in the main village, some changes were slowly happening. First, some villagers brought a pearl or two to the distribution, as gifts for the fishermen. After just a few days, one could hardly get a good fish without giving pearls.

Some families didn't have pearls. They then offered other items in exchange for fish. For a short while, the bartering culture prevailed and such a poor fisherman was suddenly the proud owner of a toy or crib; although, he didn't have kids. That soon changed, though, and pearls became the common currency. It went like that: The owner of the toy offered it for sale at an asking price of a certain number of pearls, as many pearls as he needed to get the fish. When the fish supply dwindled and he still hadn't sold the toy, he had to reduce the price to feed his family. When the number of pears received did not match the fisherman's asking price, he owed some, to be settled the following day.

Some of the fishermen started collecting oysters in the shallow waters and checking them for pearls. For that reason, fewer of them were still fishing. Fish became more expensive by the day.

Wayne's buying and selling of pearls had created rich and poor families. Families that had pearls, but had restrained from buying T-shirts or other items from the whites, were rich now.

Others had received clothing, shoes or, in one case, a magnifying glass for their pearls but wished they had kept them for getting food. Some tried to sell these items back to Wayne in exchange for pearls, but with the boat back, he wanted to hang on to as many pearls as possible. If he offered pearls at all, it was for a smaller number than he originally received for the same article, with the intent to buy them back for even less.

Taos was very unhappy. He felt he was the big looser in all these changes. If that motor boat had not re-appeared, he would have been the richest person in the village. He would have had a coconut shell full of pearls, probably all the pearls in existence. He would have set the price for fish and the fishermen would have had to accept it.

As it was, Taos had an unfinished outrigger canoe that he didn't need since he didn't fish. He was a land dweller and never went out to sea. The trees were his environment, not the waves.

He had offered the canoe to the fishermen, but nobody needed it. They all had all the canoes they ever wanted. Besides, with what would they have paid for it. Lately, they had received some pearls for their fish and were now able to buy the items from their neighbors, those which the neighbors had bought from Wayne. The canoe, however, was too big to be bought for just a few pearls. To buy the canoe, it would have taken all the pearls in circulation, a coconut shell full of them, as many as Wayne had agreed to give to Taos.

There never had been any legal disputes about possessions on the island. It was very well known what every family owned. These were the bare necessities and the barter system had pretty much evened it out over the many years and over several generations. In legal disputes, the party shortchanged in the deal is normally compensated with money. Well, there had been no money. Now there was.

After lengthy consideration and some sleepless nights, Taos decided for himself; he had something like a contract with Wayne to build a canoe. It was not conditional on having or not having a motorboat. He would finish the canoe, launch it to prove its seaworthiness, and then ask Wayne for payment in pearls. He, Taos, would be the richest person on the island after all.

To tell this to Wayne, Taos needed Henry for translation. He found both at the distribution. Henry listened to Taos' argumentation. Two thoughts came immediately to mind. First, Taos was right. He had nothing to do with the whites' means of transportation. He had a fix order for a canoe. Second, there was no way Wayne would let go of the pearls now, since they didn't need the canoe anymore because, at the same time, they had better transportation not only for the people but also the pearls.

Henry did explain to Wayne what Taos wanted but got just a head shake. What to do? Eventually, they decided to ask the master, thereby proving, again, how everything was still controlled by him.

After the opening ceremonies, with a drink, the master listened to the problem, which Henry presented in both languages. The master scratched his head and fell into deep thoughts. All three visitors could clearly see on his face how seriously he took the matter.

It was all show, though. He had worried for some time about that pearl business but didn't know what to do about it as long as the whites were still there. He knew, even if Taos got the pearls, he would not be rich but would remain the hard-working boat builder and carpenter. After Wayne's departure, those pearls would be absolutely worthless here on the island. There would not be enough goods to buy for the hundreds of pearls. Their value would go down faster than the sun sets and there would be a whole lot of unhappy citizens. Those pearls had to disappear and Wayne was the man to take them away.

Finally, the master decided; Wayne did indeed owe the agreed upon payment to Taos. This was a matter of fairness. The master's reputation was at stake and he had been fair in all these years. Before Wayne could shake his head again, the master added, "Payment should not be in pearls but in a decent sized fish for Taos every second day. He, the master, would guarantee it." Taos agreed because fish is what he wanted to buy with the pearls anyway. The master made a mental note, to not forget to increase the number of fish in the daily delivery to him by the fishermen.

After the visitors had left, the master was deep in thought. He was very concerned about the future of the community after all the changes caused by the whites like this introduction of wealth, the pearls as currency, and the equality of women, among others. In the one area where he wanted a change, which was to have more Caucasian features and fairer skin in his family, no improvement was guaranteed.

These weren't his only worries. There also was the medicine man and his revolution. Had he made mistakes in the past? Should he have killed the whites? Should he not have banned Henry? All too late now.

CHAPTER 27

One sunny day, the medicine man figured it was time for the leadership change. The whites were not yet leaving and he didn't want to wait any longer. He got everybody together for a march up the hill to fire the master and chase him and everybody else out of their comfortable quarters. He walked up front, followed by a group of battle-ready men. The spy was among them but did not yet have a plan of how to turn the crowd around. Behind followed the women and children who wanted to witness this colossal and, until a few weeks ago, unthinkable event. Rona was among the women but had no plan, either.

There was no way the refugees up on the hill, together with the family, could win a fight against this angry crowd. The question was how angry this crowd was.

The master was told they had no weapons. Order from the medicine man. He, too, knew very well how disastrous the fight of their ancestors in the original village was. He wanted to govern all present villagers, not only survivors of a battle with weapons. The master, on the other hand, figured, without weapons, there was a good chance of bluffing his way out of the situation again.

Adam watched the crowd coming closer by the minute. He knew taking away the present master's power and installing it on the medicine man would not change anything. The island would remain a dictatorship. If he only could speak the language. Adam had never learned to give speeches. In his short life as a foster child, nobody would have listened to him, anyway. But, here, he saw his chance to bring real democracy to a people. Not just to talk about it, as in the youth group back home, but to introduce it.

He ran down to the first group coming up, the men, and planted himself firmly in front of the medicine man, stopped him, and called for Rona to come forward. If he had been a villager, the medicine man or somebody close to him would have simply pushed him aside. Faced by one of the whites, it took a few minutes for the medicine man to decide how he could get rid of this obstacle. Luckily for Adam, and as it turned out for the whole village, Rona came quickly. She had no idea what Adam had in mind, but every action was better than no action.

With Rona, his lover, next to him, Adam shouted, "Neighbors, friends!" in the local language. That was a surprise to most people as well as to Rona. "I'm going to say something in English now. You have to translate."

"But the people are not supposed to know I speak English," Rona reminded him.

"So what? If they carry out what they are about to do, the master will be out of office and won't need you and your English anymore."

Just when the medicine man's patience with this interruption was about to run out, Adam started again; this time in English, "Villagers!"

Rona positioned herself more visibly next to Adam and started to translate. She was well liked in the community. For many years now, she had cared for the sick and elderly. That was very much appreciated and, overall, she was one of the nicest people on the island. So, everybody listened to what she had to say. The women had caught up by now with the men. They all realized what Rona was saying in their language was a translation of Adam's speech, but coming out of Rona's mouth gave it even more weight.

"Villagers, you are living here in paradise." Despite their slight difference in Christian beliefs, they all knew what the paradise was. "I come from one of the big cities, which by now you all have seen in Mena's book. Believe me, it's much better here." Adam said this in a very convincing way, because he believed it himself. "There is just one thing the people in this book do better than you, and that is governing themselves. They choose somebody, out of their middle, to be the master for some time. If he is good, he can continue as master. If not, somebody else is chosen by you, the people." He added, "What they don't have is the evaluation of the work done at the end of a term. I wish they did. We, here, will extend this trial to include the master, to hold him responsible, too, not just the chiefs."

At this point in the speech, the medicine man started to get nervous. "We are quite happy with our system, when we have an intelligent and well-meaning master. All you have to do is to replace this cheating master with somebody better." He started walking again, but nobody followed.

"Tell us more about this system," somebody shouted.

"Each clan picks a candidate and on the day of the election, all adults in the community walk to the village of their favorite candidate. At sunset, on that day, all the people at every village are counted. The candidate of the village with the most people present, it doesn't have to be the chief, becomes master for twelve moons."

"Are you coming or not?" the medicine man was shouting from quite a bit ahead.

"I don't think we are ready," somebody called back. "We haven't picked our candidates yet." The spy had found his role in the drama.

At that point, Adam knew that at least some people got it and would educate the others. He would help, together with Rona, because he would not have to work on the boat anymore. "There is something I forgot," he called toward the retreating crowd. "Women do, of course, participate."

The crowd stood still for a moment. The whole deal was in the balance again. Then Rona took the initiative. "Sure, I want to vote, why not. I'm as intelligent as most men." Nobody doubted that. It was the women who started walking down again and the men followed.

Adam was so proud of himself, and rightly so. He had developed a variant of democracy that did not exist anywhere in the world and, in all likelihood, had not been talked about in the lecture he had missed at the convention. It should work here, though, in the absence of ballots. It would have been easier, if the villagers had had a written language. But they didn't.

What bothered Adam, on reflection, was the missing confidentiality. Everybody would know who voted for whom. The women would pretty much vote as their husbands did. It was a start, not more, but an important one.

On the day of the vote, Adam realized, there were even more flaws in his system. The candidates in the villages were, with one exception, the chiefs of every clan, including Pug, Mena's chief. In an open vote, they could all count on getting the vote from the members of their clan. The medicine man had only the votes of his patients, not more. The opposite happened in the master's village. He was, of course, the candidate and had his large family plus the two spies, the refugees, and a few others to vote for him.

He won.

CHAPTER 28

With everything back in order and most people happy with their newly established democracy, the bishop figured it was a good time for Henry and Mena to finally get married. The wedding ceremony should take place on the hill. This was, other than the beach, the finest part of the island. Everybody was invited and everybody came.

The wedding itself was a mix between tradition and a ceremony as it would have been in the bishop's church. Everybody showed up in their finest wedding tapa, if they did have the material to make it, which wasn't always the case. Missing was the traditional pig roasting, for the lack of pigs. There was, however, lots of food.

The food was provided by the guests, indirectly. Normally, the bride's family was responsible for food and drinks. The only relative of the bride was Rona. She didn't have any food to give. She, however, was the adopted child of the master. The master was therefore closest to the bride's family. He had to provide everything for the wedding. But he, in turn, received most of his food items from the villagers. And so, it was, that the guests ate their own food. Nobody seemed to mind.

As everywhere in the world, bride and groom were asked if they wanted to get married to the other person. These questions were first put by the medicine man in the local language, and then by the bishop in English. English took longer. Much longer.

Weddings were normally carried out by the master but, as a peace offering, this time he asked the medicine man to officiate. Most people noticed and were happy that the two were getting along again.

Even though the volcano was officially extinct, as long as the villagers had lived on the island, they had always been afraid of it and not only because of the gods living there. After all, it had rumbled during their walk up the trail. The volcano had even spit out some lava, but to the other side of the island, not where the people lived. The only way to see this was from the sea, and only the fishermen did.

While everybody was up on the hill for the wedding, suddenly, the earth shook and much more than it had done previously. It happened so quickly and lasted for only a few seconds. It was over before the villagers could decide which god was angry with whom. For a while, nobody moved. When the shaking had stopped, they all continued with what they had been doing before, but their thoughts were with the volcano. A few fishermen decided to get their boats ready after the wedding on the hill was done, to see if the lava stream to the other side was thicker this time.

The master took out his scope to see if there was something extraordinary happening on the volcano. No, there wasn't, but there were too many palm trees in his line of sight to see much. They had made great efforts to hide among the dense vegetation. That was now backfiring.

About fifteen minutes later, the volcano rumbled again, and then it started spitting rocks. Big rocks and small rocks were raining down everywhere, including the area of the wedding. Everybody was fleeing in panic. Then the master's voice was booming over all the confusion and the volcano's storm-like noise, "Everybody down to the boats; fishermen get ready to take as many people as you can."

Soon ashes joined the rocks. That made it difficult for the people running to see the flying rocks and made it harder to avoid being hit. It was a total disaster. Some people stumbled and were helped up, again, by the master and his sons, who were bringing up the rear.

There was not enough space in the canoes for everybody. Some were overcrowded; one of them tipped, spilling everybody overboard. Others were about to leave with only two people inside. Again, the master had to step in. He chased everybody out, who was in a boat already. Then he ordered the fishermen to get into their own boats first. Then he had women and children lined up, and each canoe loaded as many people as it could safely carry.

Everything happened very quickly. There was one major oversight, though. During the wedding, Rona had volunteered to babysit the youngest children, those not seen old enough to take part in the wedding ceremony or whose parents just wanted to have a free afternoon to enjoy themselves.

These parents were now desperate to get their children, but where were they? Rona had taken them on a walk, playing games and having fun. She was very good at that. But now, where was she? Next came two older kids telling everybody at the dock that Rona was lying on the trail and wouldn't move.

As soon as Adam heard that, he was running toward where the kids had come from. He found Rona unconscious and bleeding from a head wound. There was no time to lose. He picked her up and carried her to the boats, all by himself. Other people were on the trail now, but they were all looking for their kids—no help to carry the lifeless woman. Adam was slightly built, and under normal circumstances would not have been able to carry her while running to the boats. Now he was.

Not everybody found space in the boats. The first batch was prepared to leave, but where would they go? Again, the master took over. Up on the hill at the wedding, he had already noticed one side of the island was not as greatly under the constant stream of ashes, due to the strong wind, probably created by the eruption itself.

"Take everybody to the cave on the other side," he shouted. This was the spot where the motorboat was once hidden. "Then come back and take more until everybody is safe." The motorboat was not of much help. It didn't start and that should not have been a surprise, after not having been used in such a long time.

Eventually, everybody was in the small cave. The last ones to leave from the dock saw the huts burning and fire spreading from there. With those gone, every sign of civilization had disappeared.

Rona was made as comfortable on twigs and grass as possible. The medicine man as well as the master and his wife were trying to get her out of the coma. She was breathing, but that was all. Adam was sitting on a stump next to her but didn't know what to do, either. Never before had he felt his deep love for this woman as strong as now, when she was about to slip away.

Everybody was sitting there, exhausted, and that, for once, included the master. It was impossible to go out onto the open water with the whole flotilla and besides, they could not all go together and, therefore, nobody did.

Suddenly, they heard the otherwise terrible sound of the motorboat, but now it was music to their ears. How many people could it hold? Was it enough, together with the canoes, for all of them to leave? Was the motor strong enough to tow them? Should they even try to leave, with rocks still falling on the water? They couldn't believe it, when the sound slowly faded away. The white men's shiny boat, with two whites inside, was not coming. Everybody looked at Adam, who stared a hole into the ground in front of him. Nobody said a word. Sometimes they heard strange sounds, mostly from above but muffled in their cave due to the solid rock walls. They didn't recognize them and had no idea where they came from.

They realized their situation was rather hopeless. For decades, they had avoided being discovered by the rest of the world; how could they now count on being discovered and rescued in a hurry, before it was too late? The long-term future, if they somehow made it, wasn't much better. They could rebuild the villages, but nothing would grow in the thick layer of ashes. Many of them thought of the similar situation their ancestors had faced so many years ago.

Whatever else happened, there was one positive aspect, as the master and the medicine man knew very well. There definitely were no gods or ancestors or anybody else in the crater of that red-hot volcano. If something was surviving, it would be the devil. Nobody suggested devil worship. The two men silently made their peace.

CHAPTER 29

Meanwhile, at RCCNZ command, all hell broke loose. Airplanes were ordered to take off and have a look at that misbehaving volcano. Ships were advised to change course. Satellites were zooming in on the event. The media had to be informed and they in turn sent out choppers and planes to take pictures for the world to see.

All of those involved concluded that no inhabited land was affected. The outbreak was the well-known natural event that had happened so often in the past in this region and would happen again. Nothing new and nothing special. This volcano was known as highly active. Official warnings had been issued from time to time not to go there.

RCCNZ did their routine work, although there appeared to be neither search nor rescue necessary. Only Bill, in his temporary job at head office, wasn't sure.

Bill knew his brother Wayne was in the area. He had almost joined him, if it hadn't been for that stint at this central station. He did not know what island exactly Wayne and the others went to, but he knew it was near the outbreak and it was volcanic. Again and again, he searched the chart for volcanic islands and found that the one currently erupting was the only one. There was no sign of people, though. The whole population of a village, in which Henry claimed to have lived, would easily be seen from the air but wasn't.

The volcano was slowing down. It still spat ashes but not with as many rocks. The tension at head office lessened. Bill's boss ordered him to get a little shut eye but remain in the station. His boss took over the ongoing communication. Not much had to be done except reminding all the official observers, as well as the media, to give the volcano some berth, not to get too close.

They all obeyed, more or less, except for one little motorboat that was running circles much too close to rocks and ashes. Bill's boss ordered a helicopter to dive down, hover in front of the boat, and scare them out of the forbidden area. A dangerous maneuver for the chopper because of the ashes that obscured their sight, but lives had to be saved at all costs.

The chopper approached the two men in the boat, who were dancing around and pointing toward the island. That was the wrong direction. Away from the volcano was the command. Unfortunately, the deafening sound of the helicopter's motor made verbal communication impossible. When the chopper was hit by a small rock, the pilots decided it was time to quit. A last glance at the boat showed the two persons were somehow resigning, one on his knees, obviously praying. Then the two boaters started running their circles again.

About two hours later, Bill got up and was briefed by the SARO, his boss. Everything was under control, except for the wild motorboat, still running in circles and half circles. Bill had a look at the monitor. One half of a circle to the left, then half a circle right, followed by a full circle and back to the half circles. No doubt the boat was writing SOS on the surface of the water. That's what these crazy circles were. He ordered the government chopper to zoom in, and immediately he recognized his brother Wayne. The other person was probably the bishop, whom he had never met personally but heard of.

"It's not about rescuing two people anymore; there is a whole tribe in danger," Bill told his boss.

"Why would that be? The island is not inhabited."

Bill was one hundred percent sure now. "It is. I know it from Adam, and he from Henry, and my brother Wayne is in that boat."

Bill's boss didn't believe it at first. His colleague had only awoken minutes ago and must have dreamed all of that. However, all rescue organizations have to follow every lead even the slightest one. When Bill stuck to his story ten minutes later, it brought the huge NZ rescue network quickly into the search and rescue mode for which it had been set up. The SARO switched the system into a major rescue operation with the lives of up to one hundred people at stake.

CHAPTER 30

Wayne and the bishop saw the chopper coming back. How could they signal this time more clearly that there were people on the island? Again, the helicopter was hovering above them. The door opened and one of the pilots, hanging on a cable, came down to them. He knew already from head office there was supposed to be a village on the island, but where? The problem was the two men in the boat had no idea where the villagers were hiding. If they wanted to be found, they would have shown themselves to the many choppers and planes long ago. But there was this fear of flying objects. All they could tell the pilot was that the villagers were probably sitting somewhere in their canoes, waiting for the volcano to stop, but then what?

The visitor from above was lifted up again and the chopper left. It would have had to fly too high to find somebody hiding in the trees and bushes. Lower down with better sight of the ground, they would have had to fly through the ashes, with the risk of being hit by rocks again. To make the situation worse, at least in the eyes of the two boaters, their outboard motor was suddenly out of gas. They were now drifting helplessly on the churning water, away from the island. Soon they only saw the top of the volcano; the rest of the island was hidden behind the curtain of ashes.

What the boaters did see next was a big, grey ship coming toward them as close as the shallows would allow it. When it was close enough, a motorboat, much bigger than theirs, was released from the bow. It was coming straight for them, and without any comment, the crew plucked the two men out of their tiny boat. Empty, it slowly drifted away. Saving a little fishing boat was not part of this mission for the navy.

To the great surprise of Wayne and the bishop, the sailors didn't take them to the navy ship but were racing with them ahead toward the island. "We want to find the people in their hiding place," the commander said, "and we need your help. You know the island better than us."

The traffic in the air had tremendously increased. There were more helicopters, some with a red cross painted on the side and the belly. The landing boat they were in passed two commercial ships that were stationary, in case they were needed.

When the fast boat was about two hundred meters from the island, rocks fell quite close to the boat. The sailors were in full protective gear. For Wayne and the bishop, they had helmets but nothing else. They tried to protect the passengers with tarps and were piling up some ammunition boxes for cover, but, on the other hand, they wanted them to see and guide the boat. A balancing act.

Luckily, it didn't take long before they found the villagers in the cave. To them, the soldiers must have been those devils out of the UFOs, which they had watched flying over all these years. For a short while, it looked like some of the natives wanted to run away, but when they recognized Wayne and the bishop, they didn't.

Not to lose any time, about a dozen, mostly mothers with children, were loaded into the speed boat, and off they went. With its powerful engine, it was within minutes out of the danger zone. The canoes would have been in danger of being hit for hours. The boat was soon back again to take the next batch aboard. So it went, until they all had been picked up. The whole operation had to be carried out as quickly as possible, since nobody knew what the volcano was still capable of. Others in the past had blown up and disappeared in the ocean altogether. An event that nobody would survive.

Henry and Adam were in the last group that was taken into the navy boat. They both had constructed a primitive stretcher, on which they carried Rona, who was still unconscious. "If she only had worn such a helmet as the rescuers had," Adam was thinking.

All the time, he and Henry wondered where the people were taken to. Now they saw it. To their great surprise, it was the same container ship that had taken them to their starting point. For Henry, it would be the third stay on that ship.

When all the villagers plus the whites were on board, and Rona in the sick bay, the soldiers left in their boat. The captain of the freighter asked Bill at RCC where to take the load. Bill didn't know. All he could say was the government would pay for the transportation, but with luck they would decide to remain together and he would have to stop only once.

The captain asked the master who had an idea. He gathered all the villagers around and asked, "What do you think about going back to the place our ancestors came from so many years ago? Would it not be nice to go home again? Maybe we will find relatives; maybe we will find the graves of our forefathers and mothers." He quickly added the female side, tuning into the new trend of equal rights for men and women. Almost all of them agreed. None of the rescued villagers had ever lived there, but somehow it felt like "going home."

The captain liked the decision, too, since that big island with the church, which at the time of the exodus was several days of paddling away, could be reached in just three hours with his ship. There, he could get rid of these savages and continue his round trip as usual. He started calculating how much he could charge the government for the waiting time and the detour.

CHAPTER 31

When the freighter arrived at the pier of the village, now grown to a town, a huge crowd was waiting for them. The ship had been fast to get there, but the media was faster. The local TV station had not broadcast anything else after it was clear the former citizens were coming back

Henry was overjoyed when he saw his parents standing at the pier. His parents, seeing him, fell to their knees, thanking God. Later on, much later, when they compared their journeys, they were quite sure the two canoes would have met. The parents' plan would have worked out if Henry had not been picked up by the freighter.

Not everybody was jubilant, though. Some present inhabitants feared the families of the former refugees would claim their land back, and not only that, family feuds of long ago would break open again, political realities could shift and carry new people into power, with the new members of the community now eligible to vote. None of that happened, at least not in a big way, with the exception of the master, who soon was elected mayor, although his former villagers were only a small minority in town.

One major factor in keeping the peace was the fact that nobody owned land privately. The government owned it and leased a few acres to every male citizen over sixteen years of age. Luckily, enough land was left, despite the increase in population, to extend this practice to the newcomers. Donations were pouring in from around the globe, which helped the new arrivals to build houses and buy equipment. A shiny new car was seen as equipment, and that excited most of the young men, who had never seen one before, let alone driven one.

The bishop learned he had been dismissed because he had neglected his duties. A successor had been installed. That didn't come as a surprise. On the positive side, the hearing about his relationship with foster children was cancelled. When the local high school was looking for additional teachers, the bishop applied and was accepted. He was very well liked by his students, although, strangely enough, he refused to do extracurricular work with the young boys. He did offer Bible studies, but only for girls. He was fighting to remain on the right track.

Henry was ready to stay on this island together with Mena and Reila, since Mena had been adamant not to be part of the crazy life in a big city, which she had seen in the photo book. Just when Henry made arrangements for their stay with his parents and the other villagers, Mena changed her mind. She still didn't want to live in such a big city but she wanted to see where Henry had been living those two years.

Where would they live in this slightly bigger town, where Henry had lived with the bishop on this far away island? The only place Henry had ever stayed in was the old garage of the church. He asked the bishop if he could go back there, at least for a while. The bishop had, of course, no say in the matter anymore, but he wrote to his successor, recommending Henry and his young family.

The new priest didn't have authority over the property, either, but he asked the administration. Back came not only an okay but also funding of up to five thousand for renovations. A kitchen was most important. There never was one in this building. The money wasn't enough to hire tradesmen, but it was sufficient to buy materials, if Henry and Mena did the work themselves. Some church members were helping them. Everybody seemed to be a shade nicer to them than expected, because they all had learned of the volcano people, had seen them on TV, and people always want to be part of a good thing. At least for a while.

Having made the decision to live away from her fellow villagers, Mena took to city life like a fish to water. She did the shopping, learned to cook, despite, or maybe because of, all the new ingredients, and became familiar with all the kitchen utensils in no time. Best of all, she learned English almost in her sleep. Reila had to learn both languages, which she did, with admiration by everybody.

Before anybody else disembarked the ship, a Red Cross plane had taken Rona away to the hospital in the big city. Her eyes were open, but, otherwise, there was still no sign of life. Adam didn't move from her side. In the city, he didn't need a place to stay. He lived in the hospital. Sometimes he slept in the visitor chair in Rona's room but never for more than an hour. Food was mostly brought to him by the nurses, who took pity on the young lad. Sometimes he went to the cafeteria but always rushed back to the room, with only half of his plate cleared.

Goranda was the only island woman who moved permanently to Auckland, despite the pictures from there. She moved in with Wayne in his big house. They spent a lot of time in bed, continuing what they had started on the island. They had a good time. When Wayne had to leave to drive his taxi, Goranda stayed in bed most days, watching TV. She was fascinated by it. All these channels at her fingertips.

Wayne visited Rona a few times. Goranda went with him only once. The frenzy of activity in the big hospital caused her an anxiety attack.

Sometimes Goranda went out alone; Wayne didn't know where to. "Just around the corner," she said when asked, "to buy bananas and ice cream." Wayne checked, and yes, she had been in the store but only for five minutes, out of the five hours she had been away. Where did she go? What did she do?

The pearl business didn't go well for Wayne, either. Most of the pearls were still on the island, under four inches of ashes. There had been no time to take any possessions.

Rona had been wearing her necklace for the wedding celebration. It was somewhere, but even after she gained consciousness back, she could not be bothered with such trivialities, while still in hospital fighting for her life.

Wayne had a few pearls in his pocket, which he had bought during the wedding. He took them to a jeweler and was advised they were rather worthless. The shape, the color, the size, nothing was right. They had probably not grown in oysters, either, but some other mollusks. There are so many different ones, all producing pearls. He never told Rona, and she wore her necklace for many years to come. It looked good on her.

That wasn't the end of Wayne's troubles. One day, he came home and was greeted by a young man who proclaimed, from now on, he would be living there. He would sleep in the big bedroom with Goranda, and that there were enough other rooms in the house for Wayne to get comfortable.

That night, Wayne checked into a motel. The next day, he asked a cab driver colleague, the biggest Maori guy he could find, for help. When the two men got there, the intruder was in the house, and so was Goranda. "Out," said Wayne to the guy, while his friend, the cabby, was flexing his muscles. He even went through part of the *ha ka* procedure, including sticking out his tongue.

The stranger simply said, "Come," to Goranda, and together they left the house, leaving a desperate Wayne and a puzzled Maori behind.

Rona slowly recovered. When she was finally released, she and Adam were in the same predicament Henry and Mena had been in. Just like her sister Mena, Rona was scared by the traffic and all the hustle and bustle of New Zealand's biggest city. Adam's home, like Henry's, had been the church on a far-away island.

Ownership there had changed. Adam talked to the new priest, and he and Rona were allowed to move into the garage, joining Henry and Mena. There were no additional funds. That was okay with Rona. She went to work, slowly at first and then as efficiently as always. She even divided a room, to make an additional bedroom, after she had learned to work with two-by-fours, plywood, and chip rock. Mena helped when the husbands were away, finishing school.

Every Friday, the friends barbequed in the open, on the church's lawn, which Henry still kept meticulous. The two women were used to eating and living in general, out in the open. In the house, they felt closed in sometimes.

I was always invited and always came. It was so much fun, listening to their stories, reminiscent of their time on the volcanic island. On one of these Fridays, I had good news. I had been approached by Social Services in Auckland. They asked if I knew a young native woman who called herself Goranda. The police had found her among the working women in the city and booked her for having not been registered and probably being underage. She had no papers. When asked for references, she gave the bishop's name, assuming he was back here again. That's how I got the call, thousands of kilometers away. Understandably, she did not want to tell the authorities about Wayne, although he lived close by in the same city. She knew by then, he would have been in big trouble because of sex with a minor.

I asked Rona to talk to her. I figured Goranda would be more open to another woman and one from the island. The main question for Goranda was if she wanted to go back to her family. She didn't. The master was informed and accepted her decision. He knew her life would be very hard in the new town because of the strict, Christian morals. There was no discussion anymore in the new community of various forms of belief. In the seventy years, the master's villagers had been away, the word of the ancient Bible had been accepted, literally. There was no room for a temporary prostitute.

That's how she was eventually put into a Christian and very understanding family, where she was now slowly growing up, until she was ready to deal with a very demanding, modern society.

Goranda phoned Rona sometimes, when her foster family let her use their phone. Every time, she asked if it was time to meet Wayne, again, but Rona found it was too soon. Goranda knew of course where Wayne lived but had strict orders to not even go near the place.

I wrote everything down, what they talked about on these Fridays, all their adventures, their feelings and thoughts during that time on the island, and I still do, with Henry's help. He always wanted to write down his story. Now we do it together.

I am the new priest.

CPSIA information can be obtained
at www.ICGtesting.com
Printed in the USA
BVOW03s2039171117
500626BV00001B/15/P

9 781773 026961